【自序】
繪本開展出價值 教學不侷限語言

英文繪本打破了傳統教學的框架，帶給孩子多元的啟發，身為高中英文老師，繪本教學對我而言，絕對不只是語言學習這樣簡單的事，而是擴展國際視野、培養獨立思考、昇華孩子內心的媒介。本書精選十五本議題繪本，顛覆一般人對繪本的想像。好的繪本把困難的事情簡單說，藉由文字與圖畫帶領讀者領略故事背後的深意；同時，透過圖片視覺的刺激可以觸發孩子的想像，經由說故事者的描述，伴隨聽覺的引導體悟更深邃的情感，進而學習關懷、同理的心胸。本書帶領讀者開展出繪本教學的另一番奧妙。

本書精心揀選十五本適合孩童閱讀的繪本，並且分為五大議題：人物傳記、親情可貴、戰地鐘聲、性別平權以及夢想驛站，帶領讀者打破國界，認識地球各個角落曾發生的動人故事，啟發讀者重視文化差異性，進而思考台灣這塊土地也有許多亟需關懷的議題並期待付諸行動。

本書將繪本又細分為五個面向：故事摘要、大師觀點、圖像思維、批判思考及教學活動。故事摘要提供讀者以最短時間認識繪本內容；大師觀點剖析繪本中「圖、文、意」三者關聯，啟發讀者領略故事的觀點與情意；圖像思維給予讀者系統性的文本呈現，運用組織圖像作為理解故事架構的脈絡；批判思考提供思考面向，反思既有價值觀，帶領讀者體會繪本的弦外之音；教學活動則給予教學者帶領孩子認識議題的方法，讓教學者能夠帶領孩子深入繪本故事情境。

身為父母親的你，請將這本書作為親子共讀的最佳工具書，藉由批判思考單元中的問題，與孩子展開深度對話；透過親子間的溝通交流，讓繪本建構孩子獨立思考的能立，英文繪本是陪伴孩子成長的最佳良伴。作為老師的你，請將繪本教學帶入教室，與課本選文搭配，透過閱讀讓孩子敞開心胸，學習包容與接納，這些繪本將是學生愛上英文課的一帖良藥。角色是學生的你，本書將教會你如何閱讀，提供思考向度，藉由閱讀策略讓英文的閱讀不再侷限在語言的學習，培養閱讀成為你生命中不可或缺的習慣。

台灣的英文教育長期著重在文法、翻譯的累積，若能加強實用及思考的訓練，相信可提供孩子更多的能力培養，秉持自身的教育初衷，語言不單單只是語言，箇中的文化內涵及價值建立，才是教育的核心。本書所分享的繪本解析與問題思考，開啟另一種英文學習的方式，透過讀者與繪本的互動，提供想像思考的空間，主動學習建構文本意義，期待讓讀者培養出自學的能力。

戴逸群

【名師推薦】

陳方濟（新竹市磐石中學校長）

教室裡的春風

　　三十年前還在研究所念書時，在《伊洛淵源錄》中讀到了北宋理學家—程顥、程頤兄弟的故事，對於明道先生圓融會通，與學生打成一片的融洽教學氣氛嚮往不已！然而，當時正在高中兼課的我，卻也常常被老前輩們耳提面命地告誡：「老弟啊！千萬不要想跟學生變成朋友，他們會騎到你頭上去的……」三十年來，從老師到做了行政再到接了校長，如果有幸遇到一位能跟學生打成一片，也能讓學生主動學習而且收穫豐碩的老師，我大概都會在心裡暗自為他祈禱，希望他能繼續堅持友善溫馨的教育方式，不要被「學生成績」的大帽子扣到無招架之力！因為我相信：考試成績只是一時的，重新點燃學生對學習的可能性甚至是熱情，卻能讓他永遠受益！

　　逸群在磐石中學服務時開創了許多先例：他帶著一群在高中入學考試中，被英文深深傷害過的小孩玩英文繪本創作；帶著學生在臉書上用好不容易擠出來的幾句破英文，邀請同學玩「臭豆腐大挑戰」；他們師生創作的繪本還找到一所小學來聯合發表；他更帶著小孩們到漁船上拍「類鐵達尼號」的微電影，他成功地藉著活潑多變又能吸引學生的方式，誘導著他班上的孩子擺脫對英文的恐懼，藉著不斷紀錄發表學生們的產出鼓舞他們，讓他們重新燃起學習英文的信心。

　　我猜像逸群這樣的老師，應該不太會搖身一變為家長奉為救星的「升學名師」，但是我卻很肯定被他教過的學生，多多少少都能體會程顥先生的弟子朱光庭回憶他教學時所說的：「光庭在春風裡坐了一月」是怎樣的境界！也盼望這次出書，又能轉化為他繼續與學生們玩創意的養分！

車蓓群（政大外文中心主任）（三民東大高中/高職英語教科書主編）

常常自稱是綜藝咖的戴逸群老師表面上搞笑，但其實是個對教學熱情澎湃，對社會各種議題十分嚴肅的好老師！

在這一本書中，戴老師介紹了世界知名的人物、兩性平權的議題、親情的可貴和人因夢想而偉大等等嚴肅且重要的面向，進一步帶領學生思考，但卻聰明的以繪本出發，佐以自己的一些經驗分享，和巧妙的活動設計，讓同學們可以在面對嚴肅議題的討論時，比較不會受限於自己的英文程度，忘記故事中真正要探討的課題，而敞開心房投入。例如書中談到第一個念白人學校的黑人小女孩—Ruby Bridges，在每天上學時所受到的壓力和辱罵，以及她如何面對的故事。戴老師分享了自己第一天上學時的經驗和壓力，以期帶出學生的討論和分享。雖然他的經驗完全不能和 Ruby 面對的相提並論，但這樣的分享不但可以讓學生勇於說出自己的經驗，更可以比較出 Ruby 當時的勇氣和面對困境的決心，也更能夠將議題延伸到校園霸凌等重要議題！又例如 Piggybook 中探討的家事分工兩性平權的議題，在現今台灣社會仍然十分真實每日上演著。透過故事的了解和活動的設計，同學們在覺得好笑的故事發展中可能驚覺這也是每天自己家中上演的劇碼，開始感受到其中的不平之後，或許就能把這些新的理解帶回每一個家庭，然後做出小小的改變。

戴老師敢於表演、敢於醜化自己、敢於在要求學生之前先要求自己。也因為如此，在我去北大高中觀課時，看到學生上課時的參與和師生中間熱烈的交流。當然，這個流暢的課程後面是無數小時的備課和演練及縝密的研究與思考。而這一本書，就是戴老師的心血結晶！無論學生的英文程度如何，他們都可以在這本書中學到課題也學到英文！

林彥良（臺北科大應用英文系助理教授）

要教出有思考力、有國際素養的孩子，走進《繪本英閱會》的國度，大師觀點帶領孩子從不同視角看世界，展現繪本教學多元深度的風貌。

李壹明（臺北市中正高中英文教師／Magic English 魔法英語廣播節目主持人）

逸群老師透過繪本英閱會一書帶領讀者們進行英文繪本閱讀之旅，他利用圖像組織圖的設計來協助我們理解各本繪本的敘事脈絡，此外，他的繪本選材五花八門非常多元，碰觸內容從性別、階級、甚至到族裔議題，更重要的是他在這本書中設計了批判思考的問題單元來挑戰我們平常的閱讀，引導我們從 "Read the lines." 及 "Read between the lines." 逐漸地進行到 "Read beyond the lines." 的層次。繪本英閱會實在是一本英文繪本教學的指導方針，值得推薦給大家。

李偉綾（臺中家商應用外語科主任）

逸群老師深入分析繪本，提供背景介紹，提問高階思考問題，繪製故事脈絡圖，拓展了學生英文閱讀能力和國際觀，讓英語教學結合生活。這是本家長和老師可以立即上手並應用於教學的好書，是目前國內最棒、最有深度的繪本教學書！

Guy Herring（新北市北大高中外籍教師）

This is an incredibly useful, well designed book that will allow you to understand different and complex issues through the medium of picture books. No matter if you are a teacher, parent or student, there is something for everyone in this brilliant book!

林淑媛（臺北市興雅國中英文教師）

　　逸群導讀繪本，突出文字脈絡，擴張書籍版圖，更把讀者拋出天外，驀然驚嘆每一本繪本的生命彷彿地球，如此豐富繽紛。

李貞慧（高雄市後勁國中英文教師／知名英文繪本閱讀推手）

　　逸群老師精選重要議題繪本融入教學，並將其教學實務經驗藉由此書分享給大家，相信對於想嘗試繪本教學卻不得其門而入的老師來說，這本書的問世會是很大的福音，誠懇推薦。

溫美玉（臺南大學附設實小教師／溫老師備課Party版主）

　　這不僅是老師和學生教與學的最佳參考書籍，連我都覺得好受用。多元、趣味、深度、效度四效合一，中英文學習一次達陣。

柯曉慧（新竹市東門國小教師／教養不正經漫畫專欄作家）

　　一個在英文教學裡「翻新意、玩心機」的老師，用盡方法就是要你愛上英文！

阿　滴（「阿滴英文」YouTube 頻道創作者）

　　英文繪本是我喜歡英文這個語言的原因之一，希望更多學習者能從戴老師「繪本英閱會」這本書籍，找到自己喜歡的故事，進而主動去找尋更多繪本、小說來閱讀！

Contents

♥ 人物傳記

我…有夢
Me...Jane...2

勇敢小鬥士
The Story of Ruby Bridges.....................................16

世界上最勇敢的女孩和男孩
Malala: A Brave Girl From Pakistan.
Iqbal: A Brave Boy From Pakistan.........................28

♥ 親情可貴

大猩猩
Gorilla..44

勿忘我
Forget Me Not..60

我想有個家
Fly Away Home...72

♥ 戰地鐘聲

爺爺的牆
The Wall...86

鐵絲網上的小花
Rose Blanche...100

四隻腳，兩隻鞋
Four Feet, Two Sandals........................118

♥ 性別平權

朱家故事
Piggybook...132

我的公主男孩
My Princess Boy..................................150

一家三口
And Tango Makes Three.....................160

♥ 夢想驛站

花婆婆
Miss Rumphius.....................................174

樹媽媽
The Tree Lady.......................................188

一磚一瓦建學校
With Books and Bricks:
How Booker T. Washington Built a School..........200

人物傳記

- Me...Jane
- The Story of Ruby Bridges
- Malala: A Brave Girl From Pakistan.
  Iqbal: A Brave Boy From Pakistan.

人物傳記

Me... Jane

我 ... 有夢

故 事 摘 要

　　故事開始於爸爸送給 Jane 的兩歲生日禮物，一隻叫做 Jubilee

的絨毛黑猩猩玩偶，Jubilee 是為了紀念在倫敦動物園內出生的第

一隻黑猩猩而發行的玩偶，當時的大人覺得烏漆抹黑的 Jubilee 會

嚇到小朋友，出乎意料的是 Jubilee 反而成為 Jane 最珍愛的寶貝，

不論到哪兒 Jane 都會帶著牠！

　　Jane 跟 Jubilee 一起觀察小鳥築巢、蜘蛛織網、松鼠爬樹，更

學習所有後院中動植物的知識，並認真地做了精美的筆記，Jane 四

歲的時候，躲進了 Nutt 奶奶的雞舍，廢寢忘食地觀察著母雞下蛋，

時間滴答滴答過了五個多小時，當家人緊張到敲鑼打鼓翻遍全村時，

Jane 和 Jubilee 卻靜靜地在雞舍的一角，等待新生命的降臨。

Jane 很喜歡在戶外和動物們待在一起，坐在她最愛的山毛櫸樹上讀著人猿泰山和 Doolittle 醫生的故事，恰巧的，非洲叢林中也有一個叫做 Jane 的女孩正跟動物們玩在一起，夜晚時分，Jane 唸著禱詞哄著 Jubilee 上床睡覺，隔日醒來，Jane 的夢想已然成真。

而這一切的一切都從小時候的 Jane 和她心愛的 Jubilee 開始……

Photo credit:《聯合報》

大師觀點 / 不同視角看繪本

　　初次翻閱《我…有夢》這本繪本，看似只是一本介紹珍古德博士的人物傳記童書，再次品嘗後，逸群老師發現這其實是一本適合所有年齡層或從事各行各業的大家來閱讀的一本書，小時候的我們都有著天馬行空的夢想，但大人們卻常因為我們的年幼而為此貼上荒誕不羈的標籤。

　　故事中的 Jane 從小就對大自然充滿強烈的好奇心，四歲的時候躲進 Nutt 奶奶的雞舍中觀察母雞生蛋的過程，而讓家人擔心不已，珍古德博士曾親口告訴全世界這個故事，並感謝她的母親並沒有因為她的失蹤而生氣，反而是傾聽她說完母雞下蛋的故事，這也是珍古德博士的第一次動物行為的科學觀察。

　　兩歲生日時，爸爸送給她的黑猩猩玩偶 Jubilee 也奠定珍古德博士成為靈長類動物學的基礎，當世界上的爸媽都覺得女孩子會被這隻烏漆抹黑的 Jubilee 嚇到時，牠反而成為陪伴 Jane 完成兒時夢想的最佳夥伴。26 歲的珍古德踏上東非坦葛尼喀湖邊的泥土，著手當地黑猩猩的研究，這趟旅程對珍古德來說可說是完成年幼夢想的築夢之旅。

　　如今經過了五十幾個年頭，珍古德博士不斷在黑猩猩的行為研究上有重大的發現，這本關於夢想、堅持與愛的傳記繪本，記錄著當代傑出女性的成長故事，是一個溫暖細膩又鼓舞人心的繪本故事。

　　逸群老師從小的夢想就是當個搞笑藝人或是節目的製作人，如今我成為一個英文老師，擁有自己的舞台及觀眾，能夠帶給學生歡笑，同時可以設計一堂 50 分鐘的英文課程，這何嘗不是一個節目，這又何嘗不算是完成我兒時的夢想呢？

視像思考／
理解故事脈絡

Timeline
Me...Jane

4 years old

Jane and Jubilee sneak into Grandm
Nutt's chicken coo
and witness the
miracle of
a chicken
laying its
eggs.

Jane's father gives
Jane a birthday
gift a stuffed
chimpanzee
named
Jubilee.

2 years old

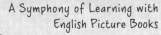

26 years old

Jane arrives in East Africa to study the chimpanzees.

Jane reads her favorite books about Tarzan of the Apes, in which another girl, also named Jane, lives in the jungles of Africa.

10 years old

批判思考／讀出弦外之音

1 **In the story, Jane received a stuffed toy chimpanzee. Do you think this had anything to do with her dream? (p1)**

故事一開始，Jane 收到一個黑猩猩玩偶，你覺得這跟她的夢想有關係嗎？

The stuffed toy chimpanzee, Jubilee, is a gift she received from Jane's father on her second birthday. Every parent thought this ugly, black toy chimpanzee would frighten their kid at that time. But Jane's father insisted on giving Jane this toy chimpanzee. Surprisingly, Jane cherished Jubilee and took him everywhere she went. Jubilee is a symbol of Jane's father's expectations for Jane. And it definitely changed Jane's life. She spent a lot of her childhood observing Mother Nature with Jubilee, with the result that Jane Goodall became a primatologist, ethologist, anthropologist and UN Messenger of Peace.

黑猩猩玩偶 Jubilee 是 Jane 的爸爸送給她的兩歲生日禮物。在當時，每個家長都覺得這隻烏漆抹黑的玩偶會嚇到他們的小朋友。然而，Jane 的爸爸反而堅持要將這隻黑猩猩玩偶送給 Jane。出乎意料的，Jane 非常珍惜 Jubilee，而且把牠當成小跟班的帶牠去任何一個她去的地方，Jubilee 其實某方面也代表著爸爸對她的期待，Jubilee 也當然改變了 Jane 的一生，她的童年在和 Jubilee 一起觀察大自然中渡過，這也讓珍古德成為一位成功的靈長類動物學家、動物行為學家、人類學者和聯合國和平使者。

2 How would you describe Jane? Cite evidence from the text to support your answer.

你會怎麼形容珍古德博士呢？從繪本中找出證據來支持你的
論點吧！

I would say Jane is a curious girl who loves nature. From the story, we know Jane used books to learn about all the animals and plants in her backyard. She even made thorough notes about those animals. Jane is also a thoughtful girl. She cherished Jubilee, taking him everywhere she went, even tucking Jubilee into bed at night. When she was a little girl growing up, she took care of Jubilee like a mother. When she grew up, she became the mother of chimpanzees: Dr. Jane Goodall.

逸群老師認為 Jane 是一個充滿好奇又愛好自然的女孩。從故事中我們
得知 Jane 認得自家後院的所有動植物，她甚至為這些動物做了精美的
筆記，Jane 也是個細心的女生，她非常珍惜 Jubilee，把牠帶在身邊，
晚上怕牠著涼會幫牠蓋被，就像是個媽媽一樣。當 Jane 長大後，她也
成為這些黑猩猩的媽媽，她就是我們敬愛的珍古德博士。

3 In Jane's message to the reader, there is a quote from Jane Goodall. "Each one of us makes a difference. We cannot live through a single day without making an impact on the world around us and we have a choice as to what sort of difference we make." Share your thoughts about this quote with us. (A Message from Jane)

在珍古德給讀者的一封信中寫道，「我們每一個人對這世界都能有所改變，我們活著的每一天都要對這世界有所貢獻——而我們擁有選擇變好或變壞。」跟大家分享一下關於這段話你的想法吧！

A man of great talents will surely be given a great task. Even though you are just a normal person, you are still unique. Each one of us can make a difference. Take Chen Shuju, for example. Poverty is something Ms. Chen has struggled with almost all her life. After her mother died during a difficult childbirth, she quit school to help support her family. Her brother died a few years later, also because her family couldn't afford proper medical care. Instead of getting angry, those tragedies inspired her to help the less fortunate. She is a vegetable hawker who works up to 18 hours a day, 6 days a week. But no matter how much she earns, she spends no more than 100 NT$ per day on herself. With the rest, she helps others. Not

all philanthropists are rich. People are regarded as great
people not because of the price, but rather the value.
Money is only useful if you give it to people who need it.

有才之能必將被賦予重要任務。但即使你只是一個平凡人,你依然是獨
一無二的,我們每一個人對這世界都能有所改變。舉可敬的菜販阿嬤陳
樹菊為例,貧困是陳女士一生都在對抗的事情,她在母親難產身亡後,
休學幫忙撐起她的家庭,她弟弟也在幾年後不幸去世,同樣是因為她的
家人無法負擔適當的醫療照顧。然而陳樹菊不但沒有變得憤恨不平,這
些人生的考驗反而激發她去幫助那些更不幸的人。陳樹菊一天賣菜長達
18 小時,一週工作 6 天,但無論她賺多少錢,她一天不花超過 100 元
在自己身上,剩下的收入,她就拿來幫助別人。並非所有慈善家都是富
有的,一個人之所以偉大不是因為他的價格,而是他所彰顯的價值。錢
財只有在你給需要的人時才真的有用。

教學活動

　　在進行《我…有夢》的繪本教學時，老師或家長可以準備一隻黑猩猩玩偶，一面和孩子共讀繪本，一面使用角色扮演的方式演繹故事。像是在逸群老師的課堂中，我就扮演起故事中的 Jane 和黑猩猩演起對手戲，讓繪本的講述更為生動。在和孩子共讀繪本時，也請老師或家長留點時間給孩子，在每讀完一個頁面時，讓孩子預測故事的發展，這樣的教學策略是為了培養孩子成為一個主動的閱讀者，學會不斷思考和預測的閱讀策略，並刺激孩子那無限的想像力。讀完整個故事後，配合圖像思維的時間軸，請孩子和黑猩猩互動，將整個故事演出，從中也可以瞭解孩子是否有理解整個故事喔！

翻攝自：Me…Jane

Me…Jane《我…有夢》
文／ Patrick McDonnell
圖／ Patrick McDonnell
出版社／ Little Brown & Co (2011)
相關影片賞析／
https://youtu.be/99gJKzlNNow
https://youtu.be/LKyrLFyOi04

延伸閱讀書單：

●中文版《我…有夢》（格林文化）

●《黑猩猩的好朋友》（維京出版）

●《黑猩猩的保母：少女珍古德》（文經社）

The Story of Ruby Bridges

勇敢小鬥士

故 事 摘 要

　　Ruby Bridges 的故事發生在 1960 年美國的紐奧良，當時美國正面臨黑白種族藩籬矛盾衝突不斷的年代，儘管聯邦政府盡力要打破種族界線，促進族群融合，但在某些地區黑白對立的情勢依舊明顯，官方為了突破瓦解當地黑白之間的藩籬，選定了四位成績優異的黑人小女生進入白人學校就讀，其中三位小女生被送到 McDonogh 19 小學就讀，6 歲的 Ruby 則進入 William Frantz 小學就讀，此舉讓那些白人家長們無法接受，他們為了避免自己的孩子跟 Ruby 同班，迫使學校將他們的孩子轉班，甚至還聚集在校門口對一個僅僅 6 歲的小女生辱罵，丟擲東西，並高舉 White Only 的標示牌，然而紐澳良的警察卻沒有出來維持秩序。當時美國的總統 Dwight Eisenhower（艾森豪）只好派出專屬侍衛天天護送 Ruby 上學，Barbara Henry 老師也非常有耐心地教導班上唯一的學生 Ruby，其他學生都因 Ruby 的關係而轉至別班就讀了。一日，Barbara 老師看見 Ruby 似乎在與這些失去理性的家長溝通，其實 Ruby 只不過是在為他們祈禱，祈求神能寬恕他們的一切咒罵，在 Ruby 父母的鼓勵與打氣下，這位勇敢的小鬥士不向挫折低頭，她的堅毅、執著與信念最後終於突破了黑白之間的藩籬。

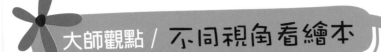

大師觀點 / 不同視角看繪本

聯合國在 1948 年的世界人權宣言 (The Universal Declaration of Human Rights) 第一條就提到：「人人生而自由，在尊嚴和權利上一律平等。他們賦有理性和良心，並應以兄弟關係的精神相對待。」然而在現實生活中卻是何等的困難，人類可以訂定法律要求人人平等，但卻無法要求每個人能打從心底尊重他人，種族、膚色、省籍是人類永遠的課題。

逸群老師看了這本繪本後，我問了媽媽我第一天上小學的情形，沒想到答案令我無法置信，媽媽說我躲在她的身後哭喊著我不要上學。看看繪本中的 Ruby，她除了得面對新學校新生活的陌生，還得穿越一群對她叫囂的不理性家長才能到達班上，別忘了，Ruby 還是學校中唯一一個與其他同學膚色不同的黑人。逸群老師真的是由衷佩服 Ruby 的勇氣。

　　Ruby 在回憶她第一天進入 William Frantz 小學就讀的情況時說到，其實她當時以為這是一場歡迎她入學的嘉年華會，經過多年後她才了解自己的角色在歷史上的意義，面對那些失去理性的抗議者，她已經忘記她到底禱告了些什麼，她只記得媽媽跟她說過，遇見無助時，只要禱告一切都會過去。然而經過這麼多年，至今她碰到無助時唯一不變的事情還是禱告。

　　在 Ruby 通過考試成為能夠進入白人學校的黑人小朋友時，Ruby 的爸爸起初是反對的，但 Ruby 的媽媽認為她的孩子需要一個更好的教育環境，而且進入白人學校這件事對非裔的美國小朋友來說是非常重要的第一步，Ruby 求學的道路是一條辛苦的道路，有著排山倒海的反對，Ruby 媽媽若無絕對的堅持、毅力與信念又怎能陪伴孩子走過那段歲月，小小年紀的 Ruby 在媽媽的陪伴與鼓勵下慢慢長大，爸爸也從反對的角色轉變為絕對的支持，這是家庭環境教養給Ruby最好的禮物。

　　在我們深深地被真實故事中每個曾經為黑白種族融合呼籲奔走的的人所感動時，反觀我們身處的台灣，即使我們是同文同種同膚色，每到選舉時卻仍要追根究柢的分界出祖先的差異或抵台的時間早晚，區分你是原住民抑或是新住民，或許在看完 Ruby Bridges 的故事後我們能珍惜身處台灣的幸福，這條省籍和族群的鴻溝不再因選舉而撕裂，畢竟我們都是最美風景台灣人。

US President Barack Obama, Ruby Bridges, and representatives of the Norman Rockwell Museum view Rockwell's "The Problem We All Live With," hanging in a West Wing hallway near the Oval Office. July 15, 2011. Ruby Bridges is the girl in the painting. Photo credit: 達志影像

Character Profile
Ruby Bridges

Who
Ruby Bridges

Where
New Orleans

When
1960

What
A 6-year-old black girl was sent to William Frantz Elementary School, a white school.

Conflict

What kind of problem did Ruby meet?
White parents thought black kids shouldn't
go to a white school. They gathered outside
the school and protested against it.

Feeling

How did Ruby feel at this
point?
Ruby didn't know what
happened. She just hurried
through the crowd and
said nothing.

Reaction

How did Ruby react?
She prayed for the people
who hated her.

批判思考 / 讀出弦外之音

1 **Who was Ruby Bridges? What made Ruby so different from everyone else?**

Ruby Bridges 是誰呢？是什麼特質讓 Ruby 和其他人不一樣呢？

Ruby Bridges was an African-American girl, who entered a white school in New Orleans at the age of 6 in 1960. She was the only black girl to come to William Frantz Elementary School. She had to face a crowd of angry white parents who shouted at her every day. However, at the time, Ruby thought it was a parade celebrating her ability to enter a new elementary school. Therefore, she just passed through the crowd quietly. Encouraged by her teacher, a white woman from the North named Barbara Henry, and her mother, Lucille, and with her own quiet strength, Ruby eventually broke down a century-old barrier. This was really a significant moment in the civil-rights movement.

在 1960 年，Ruby 是第一個進入到紐奧良白人學校的非裔美國小女孩，當時的 Ruby 才六歲，她也是唯一一個在 William Frantz 小學的黑人小女孩，她每天必須要面對一群憤怒的白人家長對她的叫囂。然而，Ruby 當時以為這只是一個慶祝她入學的遊行。因此她只是安靜地穿越這群暴民。在白人老師 Barbara Henry 及媽媽 Lucille 的鼓勵之下，和自己安靜的力量，Ruby 終於打破了一世紀的種族藩籬，這也是人權運動之中意義非凡的一刻。

If you were Ruby Bridges, would you have continued going to school?

如果你是 Ruby Bridges，你會持續去上學嗎？

If I were Ruby Bridges, I would have probably asked to be transferred to another school. I don't think I would have had the courage and determination that Ruby did. I think most people are like me. We need care and companionship from our friends. Ruby's situation is similar to school bullying or being shunned in Taiwan. Although we don't have race problems in Taiwan, we do have some special or unique students in our classes. They are labeled and discriminated against by their classmates. Whether you are a teacher or a student, we should prevent school bullying or discrimination from happening in school. Learning to respect differences is something we should learn about in school. From the story of Ruby Bridges, we know that she was a shining example of somebody who was leading the way against injustice and racial segregation. Ruby's determination and faith really encouraged people to do the right thing no matter how difficult it was.

如果逸群老師是 Ruby Bridges，我大概會要求轉學，因為我實在沒有 Ruby 所擁有的勇氣和決心。我想大部分的人也和我一樣，我們都需要朋友的關懷和陪伴，Ruby 所遭遇的狀況其實和台灣的學校霸凌或排擠的現象很類似。我們身處的台灣並沒有種族的問題，但我們的班上或多或少會有些特殊或是較獨特的學生，他們常會被其他同學貼上標籤和備受歧視。事實上，不論你是老師或是學生，我們都應該防止校園霸凌或是歧視發生在校園中，學習尊重差異更是我們在校必須學習的事情。從 Ruby Bridges 的故事，我們知道她是一個對抗社會不公不義及種族隔離政策的先驅，她的故事也鼓勵著人們要不畏艱難地堅持做一件對的事情。

3 **Are you proud of who you are? What are you proud of about yourself?**

你對自己感到驕傲嗎？你又以什麼特質而為自己驕傲呢？

I am proud of who I am. I try my best to have an open mind and be respectful toward everybody regardless of race, gender or sexual orientation. We are all different and those differences should be celebrated, even as we retain our own identity.

我對自己感到驕傲。我總是保有一顆開放的心並且尊重每個人，不論他的種族、性別或是性向，畢竟我們都不同，這些差異應該被讚美，但同時我們依舊保有自己的身分認同。

教學活動

　　在帶領孩子認識這本種族議題的繪本《勇敢小鬥士》時，老師或家長可以先進行一個親子的互動活動，拿起彩色筆讓大人和孩子來場彩繪對方的藝術饗宴，接著將畫作送給對方做為彼此的紀念，接著請孩子寫下三個畫像中彼此的差異，試著詢問孩子這樣的差異是否讓你有特殊的待遇呢？逸群老師在課堂中便是藉由這樣的方式讓孩子們察覺原來同文同種同膚色的我們還是擁有許多的不一樣，但這些不一樣似乎又沒有讓我們不一樣。接著我會將討論聚焦在故事中的小女孩 Ruby Bridges，試問孩子為何膚色的差異讓 Ruby Bridges 的上學之路會如此艱辛？反觀台灣，這塊我們生長的土地上，我們又是否存在著種族的歧視？將繪本故事連結孩子的生活經驗，用故事讓我們的孩子學著同理，學習包容與學會接納。

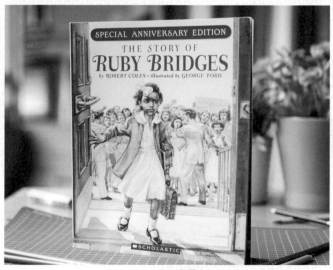

翻攝自：The Story of Ruby Bridges

The Story of Ruby Bridges《勇敢小鬥士》
文／Robert Coles
圖／George Ford
出版社／Scholastic Paperbacks (2010)
相關影片賞析／
https://youtu.be/UCTttyrCgtA
https://youtu.be/ecBORXfap9A

人物傳記

Malala: A Brave Girl From Pakistan.
Iqbal: A Brave Boy From Pakistan.

世界上最勇敢的女孩和男孩

故 事 摘 要

「讓我們不要祈禱能躲避危險，而是祈禱面對危險時能夠無所畏懼。」──泰戈爾

"Let us not pray to be sheltered from dangers, but to be fearless when facing them." ── Rabindranath Tagore

在巴基斯坦有兩位世界上最勇敢的孩子，勇敢挺身對抗大人世界中的不公不義，一個是愛讀書的 Malala，另一個是被囚禁在地毯工廠的童工 Iqbal。

Malala 出生於巴基斯坦史瓦特河谷一個名叫明戈拉的小鎮，她從小在她父親 Ziauddin Yousafzai 所創辦的學校就讀，熱愛學習的 Malala 會說一口流利的普什圖語、英語和烏爾都語，也立志想成為一名醫生救濟世人，但在宗教極端份子塔利班掌權後，女孩便失去受教育的權利。然而 Malala 並不害怕，她勇於發聲：「我有受教育的權利，我有玩耍的權利，我有唱歌的權利，我有說話的權利，我有上市集的權利，我有表達意見的權利。」「塔利班無法阻止我，

不論是在家、在學校或在任何的地方，我都還是會去上學。」「極端份子害怕書和筆，他們畏懼女性，塔利班怎敢剝奪我受教育的基本權利？」

　　Malala 極力地為女性受教權奔走並呼聲激勵女孩們重返校園。某天，在 Malala 放學的途中，一名塔利班戰士擋住了 Malala 的校車，砰砰砰地開了三槍，子彈貫穿了 Malala 的頭部，讓她的生命一度垂危。在眾人的搶救下，Malala 失去了一部分的頭骨、聽力和語言能力，但她沒有失去爭取教育的堅定，Malala 說：「塔利班向我開槍，因為他們想告訴我死亡的可怕，但他們最大的錯誤反而是教會我，就算他們傷害我，死亡卻也支持我，我活了過來，因為死亡同樣站在我這邊。」

　　Malala 的勇敢與力量喚起人們對全球近 60 萬失學兒童問題的重視，她以「巴基斯坦最勇敢的女孩」登上時代雜誌的封面，聯合國更將她的生日 11 月 10 日訂為 Malala Day（馬拉拉日），支持這位冒生命危險捍衛女性受教權的女孩。

16 歲生日時，Malala 在聯合國發表演說，她的聲音比以往更加堅定，「我不想報復恐怖分子塔利班，我想教育塔利班組織的兒女。」「一個孩子，一個老師，一本書，一支筆，就可以改變世界。」

同樣在巴基斯坦，卻有著另一個不同的故事，Iqbal 勒出生於巴基斯坦拉合爾縣邊境一個非常小的農村，他的父親向當地地毯工廠老闆借了 12 美元（約台幣 400 元），四歲時的 Iqbal 因此被家人賣到地毯工廠當奴隸，在巴基斯坦每天早上超過 50 萬年齡在四到十四歲之間的孩童得在天亮前起床，沿著漆黑的鄉間道路前往地毯工廠工作，他們每天得工作 14 小時，僅有 30 分鐘的休息時間，每天的勞動可抵扣 3 美分的貸款，但是不論多麼努力工作，Iqbal 父親所欠的債只會因利息而越來越大，工廠老闆也常不給童工們吃飯，以免他們的手指長大影響了地毯的編織，Iqbal 在 10 歲時的身高只有 120 公分，體重只有 30 公斤。

Iqbal 決定逃離工廠，並加入了巴基斯坦抵債勞工解放戰線（BLLF，Bonded Labor Liberation Front of Pakistan），

Iqbal 勇敢現身訴說自己在地毯工廠的親身經歷，他想要攻讀法律，為同樣經歷的孩童發聲，他堅決反對童工制度，遠渡重洋到美國演說：「我想要做林肯做過的事，我想要在巴基斯坦這麼做，我要讓遭奴役的孩子重獲自由。」Iqbal 幫助超過 3000 個從事勞動抵債的童工奔向自由。

家鄉地毯工廠的老闆們認為 Iqbal 已經嚴重威脅了他們的生計，在 1995 年的復活節周日，十二歲的 Iqbal 在村子裡騎著腳踏車時，一顆子彈奪走了他的生命。在他的喪禮上，有 800 個人前來參加了他的喪禮，為這位勇敢的巴基斯坦男孩默哀。

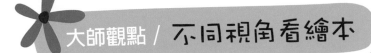

大師觀點 / 不同視角看繪本

　　Malala 的家庭是塑造她之所以能成為今日的 Malala 的重要環境，Malala 的父親從沒有回教世界傳統下的男尊女卑的概念，反而鼓勵 Malala 接受教育、表達自己想法，並告訴她去追求自己的夢想，父親會捍衛她的自由，她的母親則展現堅韌的女性力量，在關鍵的時候，一直是 Malala 最溫柔的後盾和庇護所。因為巴基斯坦錯綜複雜的歷史背景和地理環境，使得巴國情勢一直處於動盪不安的狀態裡，宗教激進人士舉著復興教義的旗幟，偏激地闡釋可蘭經的教義，使得平民百姓像是卡在石臼縫隙裡的粗糠一樣，生命只能卑微的存在。塔利班殘暴地監視控制人民的一舉一動，最後甚至關閉、焚毀學校，禁止女孩外出拋頭露面、接受教育，這對熱愛上學的 Malala 是何等的殘酷，Malala 說過：「在那些失去光明的日子裡，上學是讓我堅持走下去的動力。當我身在大街上，我有種任何從我旁邊錯身而過的人都可能是一名塔利班的感覺。」

　　台灣的孩子們可能無法想像渴望學習卻無法上學的情境，提倡男女教育平權卻會面臨死亡的威脅，而這樣的事件竟然發生在一個 15 歲的青春少女身上，台灣的社會與教育環境是幸福的，然而從學習中逃走的孩子仍然不少，透過 Malala 的故事，我要告訴這些從學習中離開的孩子，或許等我們真正失去學習的權利，才會懂得珍惜這些曾經擁有的美好，Malala 曾經說過：「我的父母一次也沒有要我放棄學業，從來沒有。雖然我喜愛上學，但直到塔利班嘗試阻止我們上學，我們才瞭解到教育的重要性。到學校上課、閱讀與寫作業不只是殺時間而已，我們的未來與之息息相關。」

　　巴基斯坦的地毯因手工精細、圖案鮮明而深受大家的喜愛，但你能想像這美麗的圖騰竟是出自稚嫩的雙手，經過沒日沒夜的工作才編織出來的，每塊地毯都沾染了隱形的血漬，血汗工廠的童工悲歌每個夜裡都在巴基斯坦的地毯工廠內響起，世界上仍有許多孩子背負著親人的負債而

從事農奴、製造工廠童工或家庭照顧工作，他們遭到不斷的剝削，薪資與勞力的不符正比造成負債永遠沒有還清的一天。

Iqbal 的勇氣與行動為這些童工帶來了希望，他為了拯救自己國家的童工，不畏惡勢力地在街頭大聲演講，他更用自己的生命換取了這些童工的自由。台灣的兒童節是每年的四月四日，那是源自於 1925 年全球 54 個國家代表在瑞士通過的「日內瓦保障兒童宣言」，此宣言承諾關懷兒童福利，包括救濟貧苦兒童和保護兒童免於危險工作。孩子們，你是否也和逸群老師一樣敬佩這兩位巴基斯坦的勇敢男孩和女孩呢？讓我們一起珍惜現在所擁有的一切幸福，也為世界上正遭遇苦難的孩童們盡一份心力。

視像思考 / 理解故事脈絡

Iqbal

1. A child laboring in a carpet factory

2. Fighting to eradicate child slavery

3. Getting shot as he resists

4. A famous quote from Iqbal:
   "I would like to do what Abraham Lincoln did.
   I would like to do it in Pakistan.
   I would like to free children in bondage."

Venn Diagram
Malala & Iqbal

Malala

1 A girl eager for knowledge

2 Fighting for education rights

3 Getting shot and surviving

4 A famous quote from Malala
"They thought that bullets
would silence us, but they failed….
One child, one teacher,
one book, one pen,
can change the world."

akistani
id

ravery

Getting
hot

批判思考 / **讀出弦外之音**

1 Why do the Taliban fighters tell the girls not to go to school?

為什麼塔利班戰士告訴女孩們不要去上學呢？

The Taliban have been condemned internationally for the harsh enforcement of their interpretation of Islamic Sharia law, which has resulted in the brutal treatment of many women in Afghanistan. Women in Afghanistan need to wear the all-covering burka. They even discourage girls aged 10 and over from going to school. Owing to the fact that 70% of the teachers are female, they are banned from working publically. Therefore, a lot of children lose the opportunity to get an education. Afghanistan has the highest rate of illiteracy in the world.

塔利班一直因過度解釋伊斯蘭教法而遭國際譴責，這也導致許多阿富汗婦女遭到殘酷的對待。在阿富汗，女性需著全覆蓋式的面紗蒙面，塔利班也禁止十歲以上的女性上學受教育，由於百分之七十的老師是女性，他們被禁止在公眾場合工作，許多的孩子也因此失去接受教育的機會，阿富汗因此成為全世界文盲率最高的國家。

2

What did you learn from Iqbal?

你從 Iqbal 身上學到什麼呢？

I learned about the bravery of speaking out against injustice and the spirit of selflessness. After Iqbal runs away from the factory, he could just hide and remain silent. But he chooses to speak out for those children who are in the same situation as him. Iqbal advocates abolishing Peshgi, which is the loan that holds children in bondage. However, threats from factory owners don't scare this ten-year-old boy. Iqbal goes to carpet factories all over Pakistan, spreading his message of freedom to over 3,000 indentured children. Unfortunately, a bullet takes his life. He sacrifices himself to get the world to pay attention to the very important issue of child slavery.

逸群老師從 Iqbal 身上學到在面對社會不公不義選擇站出來的勇氣和無私的精神。在 Iqbal 逃出工廠之後，他大可躲起來保持沉默，但他選擇為這些和他擁有相同處境的孩童們站出來，他主張廢除 Peshgi，那是一種將孩子奴役的高利貸。然而，地毯工廠老闆們的威脅並沒有嚇跑這十歲的小男孩，伊克巴勒到巴基斯坦各地的地毯工廠，傳遞自由的訊息給超過 3,000 位被奴役的孩童。不幸地，一顆子彈取了他的性命，伊克巴勒犧牲了自己喚起世界對童工奴役的關注。

3 Why is Malala in color and Iqbal in gray in the last picture?

在兩個故事最後一頁的插圖中，為何 Malala 是彩色的，Iqbal 卻是黑白的呢？

One country, Pakistan. Two children: Malala Yousafzai and Iqbal Masih. Each was unafraid to speak out. She, for the rights of girls to attend school. He, against inhumane child slavery in the carpet trade. Both were shot by those who disagreed with them. Malala miraculously survived and continues to speak out around the world. However, Iqbal passed away in 1995. That's why Iqbal is gray in the picture. Both of these two brave kids fly the kite of hope. Malala still holds it. Iqbal doesn't. The two children from Pakistan spoke out against injustice in their world. Their bravery in the face of great danger is an inspiration to all who know their stories.

一個國家—巴基斯坦，兩個孩子：Malala 和 Iqbal，他們倆位都不害怕為人民發聲。Malala 為了女性的受教權而發聲，Iqbal 則對抗地毯產業中不人道的童工奴役現象。他們倆為都不幸遭人槍擊，Malala 奇蹟式地活了下來，仍持續的在全球各地為女性的受教權發聲，Iqbal 則在 1995 年因槍擊去世，這就是為什麼 Iqbal 在圖片中是黑白的關係。此外，他們倆個勇敢的小孩在圖中正放著希望的風箏，Malala 正握著風箏，Iqbal 卻已放手。這兩位巴基斯坦的小孩站出來對抗世界上的不公平，他們勇敢面對惡勢力的行為也啓發了所有知道他們故事的人們。

教學活動

　　《世界上最勇敢的女孩和男孩》這本繪本一次介紹了兩個巴基斯坦的勇敢孩子，老師或家長不妨使用圖像思維中的維恩圖，培養孩子比較和對比（Compare & Contrast）的閱讀能力，逸群老師會運用兩節課的時間來帶領學生認識 Malala 和 Iqbal。第一節課，我會帶領孩子演出 Malala 話劇，同時共讀 Iqbal，如此一來，孩子能夠在有限時間內藉由戲劇和繪本認識兩位巴基斯坦的勇敢孩子，藉由分析兩個孩子不同的人生際遇，對角色有更深刻的認識。第二節課，孩子們則必須演出 Iqbal 話劇，透過肢體動作和戲劇演出更能深入角色心境，去體會 Iqbal 當時站出來，用自己生命來換取童工自由的勇氣。

翻攝自：Malala: A Brave Girl From Pakistan
Iqbal: A Brave Boy From Pakistan

Malala：A Brave Girl From Pakistan.
Iqbal：A Brave Boy From Pakistan.
《世界上最勇敢的女孩和男孩》
文／ Jeanette Winter
圖／ Jeanette Winter
出版社／ Simon & Schuster (2014)
相關影片賞析／
https://youtu.be/A6Pz9V6LzcU
https://youtu.be/Ctnr5pccSMY

親情可貴

- Gorilla
- Forget Me Not
- Fly Away Home

親情可貴

Gorilla

大猩猩

故事摘要

　　《大猩猩》講述的是單親家庭小女孩 Hannah 的故事，Hannah 渴望得到父親的關愛，可是現實生活中的爸爸既冷漠又嚴肅。Hannah 喜歡大猩猩，她喜歡看有大猩猩的書和看有大猩猩的電視節目，她還畫了許多大猩猩，但她從來沒有看過真正的大猩猩，Hannah 的爸爸沒空帶她去動物園看真正的大猩猩，他實在忙到沒有時間，「現在不行，我很忙，明天再說吧。」到了第二天，爸爸還是那麼忙，「現在不行，禮拜六再說吧。」到了禮拜六，爸爸又總是很疲憊，他忙到沒時間陪伴 Hannah。

　　在 Hannah 生日的前一晚，Hannah 上床的時候高興極了，因為她跟爸爸要了一隻大猩猩。夢醒時分，Hannah 發現腳邊是一隻玩具的猩猩，Hannah 要的是一隻真正的大猩猩，於是她把這隻玩具猩猩扔到牆角的玩具堆裡。當晚令人驚訝的事情發生了，玩具猩猩變成了真正的大猩猩，要帶 Hannah 去動物園玩，大猩猩穿上爸爸的大衣，戴上爸爸的帽子，一切都是這樣的合身，他輕輕的將 Hannah 抱起來，從這棵樹飛過那棵樹，穿越森林直奔動物園。

　　當 Hannah 和大猩猩到了動物園，他們發現動物園已經打烊了，於是大猩猩背起了 Hannah 翻進高牆到了靈長類動物區，Hannah 簡直嚇呆了，她從來沒看過這麼多的猩猩，大猩猩帶著 Hannah 去看了婆羅洲的大猿猴，又看了非洲的黑猩猩，Hannah 覺得這些牠們都好漂亮，可是好像都很悲傷。

　　大猩猩還陪著 Hannah 看了場電影，共享了晚餐，並在大草皮上跳了隻舞，大猩猩和 Hannah 互道了聲晚安。隔天早晨，Hannah 睜開雙眼，那隻玩具猩猩就在她的眼前，她笑了，她趕緊衝到樓下把所有的事情告訴爸爸。

　　「乖女兒，生日快樂！你想不想去動物園玩？」爸爸牽著 Hannah 的手走向前往動物園的道路，而 Hannah 的手上也牽著玩具猩猩的手往動物園出發。

大師觀點 / 不同視角看繪本

　　「父親」與「猩猩」幾乎是 Anthony Browne 作品中不可缺少的主題與元素，在《大猩猩》繪本中，Browne 描繪了一個忙碌、嚴肅、不擅言語的爸爸如何用行動來體現父愛的動人故事。同時也細膩地刻劃出單親家庭中生長的孩子，害怕孤獨、缺乏安全感、渴望父愛的心情。父親其實就是那隻大猩猩，他的外貌雖高大威武，但內心卻細膩溫暖。Hannah 夢境中的大猩猩其實就是父親完美形象的想像，大猩猩的出現撫慰了 Hannah 渴望父愛的心情，同時也讓大人重新思考親子關係，爸爸帶著 Hannah 前往動物園的實際行動更讓 Hannah 破碎的心獲得修補，手牽手前往動物園的 Hannah 此刻的心情想必是充滿著幸福，她手中握著大猩猩玩偶，更是希望父親的陪伴不要離開，畢竟在孩子的成長過程，陪伴其實就是最好的關懷。

　　《大猩猩》繪本除了探討單親家庭的教養問題，在家庭關係及弱勢兒童上的議題上也處處充滿 Anthony Browne 式的人文關懷，在繪本中 Browne 帶領著讀者優遊在現實與虛構並存的奇妙場景，啟發讀者無盡的想像空間，Anthony Browne 曾說：「我爸爸是個不尋常的人，表面堅強，內心羞澀。有點像我常畫的大猩猩。」

　　在 Anthony Browne 的早期作品中，不管是《大猩猩》中那嚴肅冷漠的父親，或是本書介紹的《朱家故事》中，好吃懶做且大男人主義作祟的朱爸爸，總是讓讀者覺得書中父親在 Browne 心中有些負面。其實這也正反映了 Anthony Browne 自己的生命經驗， Browne 在小時候與父親其實非常的親密，兩人常一起畫上好幾小時的畫，但青少年時期的叛逆，導致他與父親的關係降到冰點，也因父親在他 17 歲那年意外地過世，讓正處親少年時期，急需父親形象與引導的 Browne 非常受傷，直到成年後都無法釋懷父親在他成長過程中的缺席，這樣的情緒一直展現在他的繪本作品中。

　　多年過後，Browne 的母親搬來與他同住，帶來了一件父親常穿的睡袍，這件睡袍彷彿帶領著 Browne 回到與父親共處的時光隧道，那一刻，Browne 變回了小男孩，思念起那個和上帝一樣無所不能的父親，這個經驗使得 Browne 重新拾回對父親的美好回憶，也改變了日後繪本作品中父親的形象，他創作的《我爸爸》繪本中，父親總是穿著同樣一件睡袍，這件睡袍也安慰了成年後重新面對失去父親的 Anthony Browne。

　　猩猩的高大威武，臉部表情總帶有一分嚴肅，這樣鮮明的形象讓 Anthony Browne 常把猩猩與記憶中的父親產生連結。在他的心中，父親擁有碩大的力量，同時也有顆細膩溫柔的內心，身為一家之主的爸爸必須在小孩面前那樣的無所不能，莊重威嚴，但實際上他們和媽媽一樣，同樣關心自己的孩子。你曾經和爸爸說聲感謝嗎？如果沒有，不妨親口和爸爸說聲辛苦了，如果說過，就讓我們再和爸爸感性一次吧！

視像思考 /
理解故事脈絡

Gorilla

2

Hannah would like nothing more than to spend time with her father. However, her father was too busy to take care of her. "Not now, I'm busy, maybe tomorrow" is his usual response to her. On the eve of Hannah's birthday, she asked her father for a gorilla as her birthday present.

1

Hannah, a young girl, absolutely adored gorillas. The posters in her room, the bedside lamp, the box of cereal, were all adorned with her favorite animal. She spent her time reading, drawing or watching programs about them. But she had never seen a real gorilla.

Hannah

3 Father prepared a toy gorilla as a birthday gift for Hannah. But she didn't like it. She wanted a real gorilla instead. Therefore, she threw it into a corner with her other toys and went back to sleep.

4 Something extraordinary happened; the toy gorilla became a real gorilla at the end of Hannah's bed. They began a magical adventure. They embarked on the trip to the zoo, and saw a movie together.

5 The next morning, Hannah jumped out of bed excitedly. She rushed to tell her father about the amazing journey. Her father approached her and wished her a happy birthday. They walked to the zoo hand in hand. Hannah's dream had finally come true.

Gorilla

批判思考 / 讀出弦外之音

 1 "Gorilla" is a picture book with themes of loneliness and family affection explored through illustration as well as text. Share how you feel about these two themes in "Gorilla" with us.

《大猩猩》是一本透過插畫和文字來探討寂寞和親情主題的繪本，請和我們分享你在書中所感覺到的這寂寞和親情。

In the beginning of the story, Hannah is a young girl who desires her father's affection. But only loneness and solitude can accompany her. When Hannah comes to her father's room, her father has his back to her daughter. Hannah's isolation is also emphasized by the rectangle of light coming through an off-stage door. The rectangle forms a border between Hannah and her father. However, something peculiar happens on the eve of Hannah's birthday, a gigantic gorilla showed up at the end of Hannah's bed. Hannah's longing to spend time with her father is embedded within every page of her fantastic night-time adventure. In the end, her dream of visiting the zoo really comes true. Hannah is walking to the zoo hand in hand with her father.

在故事的開始，Hannah 是一個渴望得到父親關愛的小女生，但總是只有孤單和寂寞能夠陪伴著她，當 Hannah 去爸爸的房間時，爸爸也是背對著他的女兒，Hannah 的孤單更透過插畫中的長方形餘光特別被強調，這道長方形的光線更形成爸爸與 Hannah 的看不見的邊界。然而，奇妙的事情在 Hannah 生日的前夕發生了，一隻巨大的猩猩出現在 Hannah 的床前，Hannah 想和爸爸相處的渴望在每幅奇幻的夜間探遊中出現。最後，Hannah 也一圓和爸爸一起去動物園的夢想，她正與爸爸手牽手走向前往動物園的道路。

2 Why does Hannah think the orangutan and the chimpanzee were beautiful, but sad? (p17)

為什麼 Hannah 覺得婆羅洲大猿猴和非洲黑猩猩都很漂亮，
但卻非常悲傷呢？

In the zoo, the orangutan and the chimpanzee live behind the cage. They are feed on time by the zookeeper. When they are sick, the veterinarian will look after them. They seem to have nothing to worry about, but their expressions show that they feel sorrowful. They lose their freedom and need to live behind the bars on the first day they are sent to here. A lot of animals are sent to the zoo when they are young. They also need parents' love and care like humans, not to mention the fact that chimpanzees are the animals which are like people the most. Material can't replace love and care, but company can help children grow up.

在動物園中，婆羅洲大猿猴和非洲黑猩猩都住在籠子裡面，動物管理員定時會餵食。當生病時，也有獸醫會照顧他們。他們似乎沒什麼好擔心的，但他們的表情透露出悲傷的訊息。其實，他們在被送來這邊的第一天就失去了自由，必須過著住在欄杆後面的日子，很多的動物甚至在很年幼時就被送到了動物園，他們和人類一樣需要父母親的關愛，何況黑猩猩是動物中最像人類的動物。物質並不能取代愛與關懷，但陪伴卻可以幫助一個孩子成長。

The gorilla took Hannah to see the orang-utan and a chimpanzee.
She thought they were beautiful. But sad.

3 In "Gorilla", Hannah eats breakfast with her father in the beginning and dinner with the gorilla in the end. Do you find any differences between these two scenes? (p2 & p22)

在《大猩猩》繪本中，Hannah 在故事一開始和父親吃早餐，並在故事最後和大猩猩共用晚餐，你有發現這兩個場景不一樣的地方嗎？

Browne uses light color to portray the coolness between Hannah and her father in the scene of the breakfast. Father is reading newspaper and his expression is solemn and stern. The newspaper which is like a wall hinders the interaction between Hannah and her father. Browne tries to tell the readers their relationship is cold and apathetic. However, the light becomes brighter in the scene of dinner. Gorilla's face is kind and gentle. If you watch it carefully, a smile can even be found in Gorilla's face. Girls' favorite food, like strawberry, sundae and cakes, can be found on the table. Even the distance between Hannah and Gorilla becomes shorter. Eating dinner with Father is Hannah's dream. Gorilla is the perfect imagination of a father in Hannah's mind. Fortunately, Gorilla is the avatar of Hannah's father. She finally receives father's affection.

在早餐的場景中，Browne 用了淡色系的插畫來彰顯 Hannah 和父親間的冷漠，父親正在閱讀著報紙，他的表情莊重又嚴肅，報紙在這也成了一道阻礙 Hannah 和父親交流的一道牆，Browne 試圖告訴讀者他們的關係既冷漠又無情。然而，在晚餐的場景中，光線變得明亮，大猩猩的臉部線條也變得慈祥和藹，如果你更仔細看，一抹微笑就掛在大猩

猩的臉上，女孩兒們最愛的食物，像是草莓、聖代和蛋糕，就在他們的餐桌上，
Hannah 和大猩猩的距離甚至變得更近了。和爸爸共進晚餐是 Hannah 的夢想，大
猩猩更是 Hannah 心中完美的父親形象。幸運地，大猩猩在故事中就是 Hannah
爸爸的化身，她最終也得到了父親的關愛。

教學活動

　　《大猩猩》是一本非常適合親子共讀的繪本故事，大人和孩子都可以藉由這故事反思自己與親人的家庭關係，不知孩子心目中的爸爸形象是不是和書中的大猩猩一樣，擁有全能的力量，同時又有顆細膩溫柔的內心呢？逸群老師在課堂上會邀請學生拿起電話，透過話筒傳達對父親多年來想說卻又羞澀說不出口的感謝，這堂課中有歡笑，有淚水，有懊惱道歉，也有深情流露。大人們是否因為工作的忙碌、父親的威嚴或是不擅言詞的個性忽略了與孩子的相處？孩子們又是否因為課業的壓力、友情的維繫或是電玩的誘惑而忽略的從小照顧你長大的親人呢？讓我們從這通電話重新找回那份埋藏在心中許久的感謝。

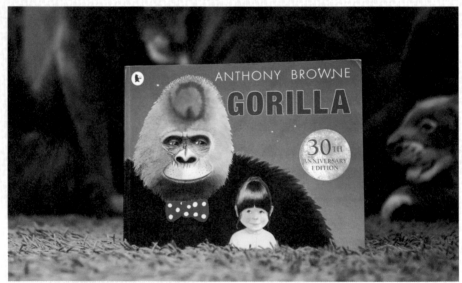

翻攝自：Gorilla

Gorilla《大猩猩》
文／ Anthony Browne
圖／ Anthony Browne
出版社／ Candlewcik Pr (2014)
相關影片賞析／
https://youtu.be/z_AguDqCBvo
https://youtu.be/CL04A-DrlEQ

寫一封信給你的父親

親情可貴

Forget Me Not

勿忘我

故 事 摘 要

　　《勿忘我》這本繪本透過小女孩 Julia 的角度敘述心愛的奶奶

得到阿茲海默症後逐漸忘記自己的心路歷程，故事的開始 Julia 記

得的奶奶依然甜美依舊，她的眼睛像極了蛋糕上閃爍的燭火。每當

Julia 到奶奶家，她都會準備 Julia 最喜歡的炸雞和手工餅乾來歡迎

Julia。和奶奶依偎在一起時，奶奶身上總是散發出肉桂和丁香花的

香味。

　　韶光飛逝，潮汐漲退，奶奶的記憶彷彿被潮水一波又一波地

帶走，起先是家人的名字，當她叫她孫女 Sally 或是 Harry 而非

Julia 真正的名字時，Julia 只能假裝奶奶只是在和她玩遊戲。但情

況每況愈下，奶奶開始忘記 Julia 和她一起經歷的事物，Julia 問奶

奶說：「記得我們一起去拔草莓那次，我跌倒在樹叢裡，全身被刺

扎傷那次嗎？」「記得當我們一起去動物園，我想要爬過圍籬去摸

大象的鼻子嗎？」奶奶全部都忘記了。

奶奶也被禁止開車了，因為她會忘記自己把車停在哪，當 Harry 叔叔去解救她時，奶奶卻說她只是想看看 Harry 叔叔俊俏的臉龐。奶奶會把鹽巴當成是糖撒在蘋果派上，家人們都不忍苛責懊惱的她。爸爸幫奶奶找了個幫忙打掃和煮飯的傭人，但每當 Hester 太太出現，奶奶以為她是小偷，便用掃把將她掃出大門。所以每當清潔日，家人總是帶奶奶去些不很特別的景點，但奶奶愛極了這樣的兜風。

在一個暴雪的早晨，Hester 太太發現奶奶只穿著睡袍在雪中挖著已經枯萎的勿忘草，她似乎忘記了寒冷。當 Julia 和媽媽去探望奶奶時，奶奶似乎也不認識他們了。Julia 問了媽媽：「奶奶怎麼了？」媽媽告訴 Julia 說：「奶奶得了一種沒人知道怎麼治癒的疾病。當我們下次來奶奶家時，奶奶就不住這了。她會被送到一個提供特殊照顧的地方，那邊住著和她同樣年紀的老先生和老太太。」

　　這聽起來對 Julia 來說一點都不好。多半時候，奶奶已經認不得 Julia 了。即使如此，Julia 還是緊緊抱著奶奶並輕撫她泛白的頭髮，她希望奶奶的眼神能回到從前，和蛋糕上閃爍的燭火一樣。當庭院的勿忘草開花時，Julia 會將這些勿忘花舖在奶奶床前，奶奶會開心的拍手就像是她以前那樣，彷彿告訴著 Julia 奶奶從來沒有忘記過她。

大師觀點 / 不同視角看繪本

《勿忘我》的英文書名為 Forget Me Not，Forget-me-not 其實就是勿忘花的英文，作者 Nancy Van Lann 用小女生 Julia 的視角和語言，敍述患有阿茲海默症的奶奶隨著時間不斷失去記憶的點點滴滴，而 Julia 則必須找到一個持續和奶奶保持連結的方式，她用把勿忘花舖在奶奶床前的方式，提醒著心愛的奶奶不要忘記她這個可愛的孫女。

Nancy Van Lann 用她細膩的文字編織整個故事，這也讓讀者在讀起這故事時有股淡淡的哀傷，但再仔細翻閱整本繪本，你會發現家人的親情及陪伴貫穿了整個故事。書中每幅插畫中的奶奶皆有家人的陪伴，在奶奶四周圍的光線也總是保持明亮，這彷彿告訴著奶奶家人始終沒有離開過她。縱使奶

奶會記錯 Julia 的名字，忘記自己的座車，將鹽巴加到本該加糖的蘋果派中，甚至將幫忙打掃及煮飯的 Hester 太太當成小偷，家人始終伴隨著奶奶，縱使最後必須將奶奶送到療養院，Julia 大大的擁抱也讓奶奶在寒冬中感受到親情的溫暖。

　　阿茲海默症最讓人痛苦的，往往是病患家屬需不眠不休的看照，以及被摯愛病患遺忘的哀傷，在繪本中你可以看見奶奶在叫錯 Julia 名字時，Julia 假裝奶奶在和她玩遊戲的配合演出，在吃到奶奶烘培的超鹹蘋果派後，全家人點外帶餐點的包容，Julia 見到奶奶在酷寒大雪中挖掘勿忘花的同情，這些家屬的情感流露忠實呈現《勿忘我》中最珍貴的親情元素，奶奶在見到 Julia 拔給她的勿忘花朵時的微笑，也讓 Julia 重新找回和奶奶的連結，我想這也是家屬在照顧病患的辛苦下，能夠持續陪伴的最大泉源。

視像思考／
理解故事脈絡

Cyclical Diagram
Forget Me Not

1

Julia's grandma used to make fried chicken and biscuits whenever Julia's family visited.

2

Grandma smelled like cinnamon and lilac when they cuddled up close.

3

As time passed, Grandma started forgetting more and more. She started to forget who her family members were.

4

Later, Grandma started to forget what she had done together with her family in the past. She wasn't allowed to drive anymore, and her cooking wasn't the same.

7 Julia would gather enough forget-me-nots to cover Grandma's quilt. When Grandma saw her bed all abloom, she would smile and clap her hands just like she used to.

6 Grandma won't live in her house anymore. She had to accept special care in a nursing home.

5 Grandma swooshed her maid with the broom. Her situation kept getting worse. She even tried to dig forget-me-nots from underneath the snow in her nightie only. She seemed not to notice the cold.

批判思考 / 讀出弦外之音

① Why does Nancy Van Lann name the book-"Forget Me Not"? (cover)

為什麼 Nancy Van Lann 將此書命名為勿忘我呢？

"Forget Me Not" is a touching story about a young girl, Julia, and her feelings about her grandma's onset of dementia. The look at the impact of Alzheimer's disease is personal and touching. Told in the first person, the book looks at the changes of Julia's grandma. In the end of the story, when Julia's family made the difficult decision to move Grandma to a nursing home, Julia mourned the change. Julia and her family had to make the best of it. Every time Julia visited her grandma, she was still her old sweet self. Julia greeted her with a big hug. She would put forget-me-nots on her quilt to remind Grandma not to forget her. Forget-me-not is a kind of flower often worn by ladies in medieval times as a sign of faithfulness and enduring love. The family affection between Grandma and Julia will be everlasting in their minds.

《勿忘我》是一個關於小女孩 Julia 和她遭遇失憶症襲擊奶奶的感人親情故事，書本觸及到阿茲海默症對於患者及家人的衝擊，親身描述的故事既動人又令人同情。全書使用 Julia 的第一人稱視角探討 Julia 的奶奶在患病後的一切改變。故事的最終，Julia 的家人必須做出將奶奶送至療養院的困難決定，Julia 為這改變感到哀痛，但 Julia 和她的家人必須做出對奶奶最好的決定。每次當 Julia 來探訪奶奶時，奶奶仍然是她那甜美依舊的奶奶，Julia 會給她大大的擁抱。她也會把勿忘花鋪在奶奶的棉被上提醒著奶奶別忘了她。勿忘花是一種在中世紀女生會配戴的花朵，象徵著忠貞及永恆的愛。在 Julia 和奶奶之間的親情也會一直持續在她們彼此的心中。

Where can you see the family affection between Julia and her grandma in the book?

你從書中哪裡看到 Julia 和她奶奶的親情流露呢？

In the beginning of the story, Julia's grandma used to make favorite foods to welcome her. Grandma smelled like cinnamon and lilac when they cuddled. But as time passed, her grandma suffered from Alzheimer's disease and started forgetting who her family members were. A little later, Grandma started to forget what they had done together in the past, but Julia and her family never left Grandma. Despite the grandma's decline, the light remains bright in the illustrations and the family stay close knit in a visual way. As a patient's relative, Julia tried her best to find a way to continue to connect with her grandma even though she couldn't remember her anymore. Julia leaned over to give Grandma a big squeeze and smooth her white hair, just like Grandma used to do for her. Grandma's spirit had already stayed in Julia's mind forever. It's a story about a young girl's unconditional love for a cherished grandma.

在故事的開頭，Julia 的奶奶總是用 Julia 愛吃的食物來歡迎她的造訪，當她們依偎在一起時，奶奶全身散發出肉桂和丁香的清香。但隨著時間的流逝，奶奶承受阿茲海默症的折磨，開始忘記她的家人。又過了一陣子，奶奶開始忘記她們曾經一起做過的事情，但 Julia 和她的家人不曾離開過奶奶。儘管奶奶的情況不斷惡化，插圖中的光線不曾暗過，家人們也緊緊跟隨在奶奶身邊。身為一個病患家屬，Julia 盡力的找出和奶奶保持連結的方法，Julia 會給奶奶大大的擁抱並輕撫她泛白的頭髮，就像是奶奶以前對她做的一樣。奶奶的精神也早已永遠留在 Julia 的心中。這是一個關於小女孩對她珍愛的奶奶的故事，一個小女孩無條件的愛。

3 **Please share the story between you and your grandma with us.**

請和我們分享你和奶奶的故事吧！

My grandma passed away several years ago. In my memorial, when I visited my grandma's house, she used to sit in an old rocking chair talking to me. "Practice filial piety to your mother, and always take care of your mother." she told me these two things every time. She only understood Taiwanese, so I needed to use my poor Taiwanese to communicate with her. Sometimes she couldn't understand what I talked about; she used her bubbling laughter to answer me. I used to sit next to her and smoothed her white curly hair and told her how adorable she was. Although my grandma had already left us, every time I saw my mom sitting on the rocking chair, Grandma seemed to come to my mind.

我的阿嬤在幾年前去逝了，在逸群老師的記憶中，每當我去阿嬤家，阿嬤總是坐在一張老舊的搖椅上和我說話，「要孝順恁阿母。要照顧恁阿母。」這兩件事是她每次都提醒我的。阿嬤只聽得懂台語，所以我必須用我破爛的台語和她溝通，有時候阿嬤會聽不懂我在說什麼，她會用她那爽朗的笑聲來回應我。我常坐在她的身邊並輕撫她泛白的捲髮，告訴阿嬤她有多可愛。雖然阿嬤已經離我而去了，但每當我看到我媽媽坐在搖椅上時，阿嬤似乎又回到我心中。

教學活動

　　《勿忘我》書中描述奶奶的記憶隨著時間一點一滴的流逝，其實在逸群老師的班上有不少孩子是爺爺、奶奶扶養長大的，這些高中的孩子在成長的過程中都有著爺爺、奶奶伴隨的痕跡，在閱讀《勿忘我》的故事前，老師或家長可以請孩子帶上爺爺或奶奶的照片，請他們用英文講一段小時候和爺爺、奶奶的故事，這些埋藏在內心深處的故事相信都會是觸動孩子心靈的養分，也讓長大後搬出爺爺、奶奶家的孩子們能一點一滴的重拾和爺爺、奶奶相處時光的記憶。

翻攝自：forget me not

Forget Me Not《勿忘我》
文／ Nancy Van Lann
圖／ Stephanie Graegin
出版社／ Random House Childrens Books (2014)
相關影片賞析／
https://youtu.be/lr3SKg3kHfc
https://youtu.be/ZrXrZ5iiR0o

親情可貴

Fly Away Home

我想有個家

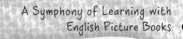

故 事 摘 要

　　小男孩 Andrew 和他的爸爸住在機場裡，爸爸跟他說住機場總比流落街頭好，不過他們得非常小心以免被逮到，Slocum 叔叔和 Vail 叔叔就被逮了，因為他們違反了住在機場的第一條守則：低調，低調，再低調。

　　Andrew 和爸爸每天都穿著藍色牛仔褲、藍色汗衫和藍色夾克，附帶一個藍色的拉鍊包包，裡面裝著換洗的藍色衣服，盡可能地讓自己看起來和普通人沒兩樣，他們穿梭在各航空公司的候機位，達美、環球、西北是他們的最愛。

　　旅客、機長、空服人員、帶著掃帚的清潔員、飛機起降、行李在輸送帶上的跳動、手扶梯的上下，機場內的一切都在不停的移動，每個人都要趕往不同的地方，但只有 Andrew 和爸爸總是留下。

有一次，一隻棕色的小鳥誤闖了航廈卻飛不出去，牠就在天花板挑高的空間拍打著翅膀，飛蛾撲火般地撞著玻璃，跌在地上喘氣，Andrew 小聲地對鳥兒說：「別放棄，你一定可以飛出去的！」連續幾天，鳥兒都垂著一邊的翅膀飛著，就在牠發現電動門打開的那瞬間，牠終於溜出去了。Andrew 喃喃自語地說著，飛吧，鳥兒，回到自己的家！雖然 Andrew 聽不見鳥兒的回應，但他知道鳥兒在唱歌，現在的 Andrew 就和自由的鳥兒一樣開心。

每到週末，Andrew 爸爸要搭公車去城裡做辦公室保全的工作，那時也住在機場的 Medina 太太就會照顧 Andrew。Medina 家中還有 Medina 奶奶跟一個小男孩 Denny。

Denny 是 Andrew 的好朋友，他們會去收集散落在機場的行李推車，因為歸還就可以得到 50 分錢的退幣。Andrew 爸爸回來時，他會為 Medina 一家買漢堡答謝他們的照顧，以前要是 Andrew 和

Denny 大有所獲，他們會買派來犒賞自己，但 Andrew 不再這麼做了，他把錢存在鞋子裡，希望能夠擁有一間自己的公寓，就像回到媽媽過世之前一樣。

　　過了明年暑假，Andrew 就得上學去了，但怎麼去呢？Andrew 爸爸也不知道，但他知道教育對 Andrew 很重要，所以他們會想出辦法解決。好朋友 Denny 已經 7 歲了，但還沒有上學，爸爸說孩子的教育是不能等的。

　　機場中常常見到人們團聚，有時候，Andrew 氣得想要推開他們，但他知道這樣做會引人注意，有時候他很想哭，他覺得他和爸爸會永遠住在這裡，這時，他就會想起那隻小鳥。牠等了一段時間，門會打開，當鳥兒展翅高飛時，Andrew 知道牠在唱歌。

大師觀點 / 不同視角看繪本

　　繪本作家 Eve Bunting 總是利用溫馨的小品故事探討各種社會議題及生命的價值觀，全書使用小男孩 Andrew 的第一人稱口吻敘述以機場為家的無奈，讓大人也能夠用不同的角度來省思現今社會的問題，本書探討的社會議題有居住正義、單親家庭及生命教育。

　　故事中，Andrew 與爸爸以機場為家，夜宿一個又一個的航空櫃台，隱喻著現今高房價產物下的無殼蝸牛們租屋度日的窘境，居無定所的日子，蝸居窄房的悲哀，更訴說著居住不正義的事實。

　　Andrew 媽媽在他早年過世，爸爸一人獨自撫養，身穿藍色衣物，隱藏自己流落街頭的事

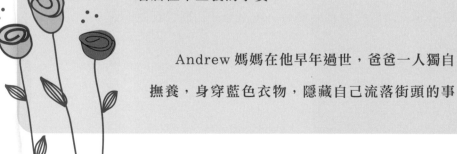

實，深怕被航警認出而被驅離的現實不也呼籲著社會需要對弱
勢的一方擁有更多的關心與關懷，Andrew 收集機場行李推車
是不是像極了為求溫飽而拾荒的街友？愛看電影的讀者會發現
這畫面，不正巧是湯姆漢克斯在《航站奇緣》中收集行李推車
獲取退幣的情節，想必編劇一定有受到 Eve Bunting 的啟發。

　　在故事的結尾，雖然單親的 Andrew 爸爸無法負擔龐大的
經濟壓力而居無定所，Andrew 見到機場團聚景象難免心酸，
但 Andrew 回想起當時闖入航廈的鳥兒展翅高飛的畫面，不也
告訴我們面對困境，心中得擁有希望並樂觀地面對未來，在《當
幸福來敲門》這部電影中，威爾史密斯和他唯一的兒子因無法
付出房租被逐出公寓，住進汽車旅館，正當情況逐漸好轉，在
銀行的存款又因欠稅被政府全數充公，父子倆只好露宿街頭，
但他堅信能夠帶給兒子更好的明天，追求滿臉笑容的幸福，於
是他從 20 名實習生中脫穎而出，成為華爾街的股票經理人，
也為自己跟孩子成就了一個幸福的家，回頭看看 Eve Bunting
的《我想有個家》繪本，頓時覺得 Andrew 和 Andrew 爸爸
充滿著希望。

視像思考 / 理解故事脈絡

Rising Action

Event 3:

Everyone i the airport was o the move. Howeve Andrew and his da stayed put.

Event 2:

A woman with a metal cart full of stuf was moved out from the airport.

Event 1:

Mr. Slocum and Mr. Vail were caught because they sang too loudly.

Resolution

Andrew believed they would get out from the airport, just like the bird, and be able to fly away home.

Exposition

Andrew and his father lived in an airport. The first rule of living in the airport was not getting noticed. So they tried to look like nobody at all.

Plot Diagram
Fly Away Home

Falling Action

Andrew's dad made a living by working as a janitor in an office. Andrew also earned a little money collecting rented luggage carts.

Climax

Once a bird was stuck in the airport. Although it kept getting knocked down, it finally got out.

79

批判思考 / 讀出弦外之音

1 What does "Andrew and his father changing airline" imply? (p6)

Andrew 和爸爸在故事中不停轉換航線，這代表著什麼呢？

It implies that they need to change to a different airline to sleep; otherwise, they will get caught. It represents the grief of the tenants who are left out in the cold. In Chinese, we call those people "Snails without Shells."

他們不停轉換航線以免被逮到象徵著當今社會高房價下無殼蝸牛的悲哀。

2 Why do Andrew and his father wear blue? What life lessons can you learn from this? (p8)

為何 Andrew 和爸爸總是穿著一身藍呢？你有從中學到任何的生活哲學嗎？

They don't want to be noticed so they try to look like nobody at all. I think they are trying to keep a low profile. Sometimes you need to squat lower in order to jump higher.

因為他們得保持低調，跟一般旅客一樣，蹲低是為了跳得更高。

3 In the story, a brown bird flies into the terminal and becomes trapped inside. After a period of hardship, it finally slips out through the sliding door. For Andrew, what does the bird in the story symbolize? With what inspiration does the little bird provide him? (p16)

故事中，小鳥誤闖航廈而被困住，幾經努力後飛出門外。對 Andrew 而言，小鳥的寓意又是什麼呢？小鳥又給了 Andrew 什麼樣的啟發？

To me, the bird is the symbol of hope. Although the bird hits the window and gets knocked down, it doesn't give up. But the bird finally finds a crack from which it can slip through and fly into the open sky. I believe Andrew is inspired by this scene. That's why he knows the bird is singing, because the bird is also a symbol of Andrew himself. And so Andrew, in his own heart, is also singing a song for the little bird. From now on, the terminal is no longer a cage; it will never be able to hold him in again.

對逸群老師而言，小鳥對 Andrew 是個希望的象徵，雖然小鳥受困航廈，在尋找出路的過程中撞上玻璃，跌坐地板不停喘息，但小鳥最終還是找到縫隙飛向屬於自己的天空，Andrew 看到此景心中一定非常感動，這也是為什麼他能聽見小鳥正在唱歌，因為小鳥代表著也是自己，此時 Andrew 心中也正唱著歌為自由的小鳥鼓舞，這航廈在也不是鳥籠，在也關不住屬於自由的他。

教學活動

　　雖然《我想有個家》一書在描述 Andrew 與爸爸以機場為家的親情故事，但其實書中也觸及目前台灣所擁有的高房價問題，老師或家長可以請孩子預設自己未來將要從事的職業，並請孩子上網查出該職業的大約年收入，接著讓孩子上網查查學校附近的房價。在逸群老師的班上，許多孩子很驚訝原來自己需要不吃不喝的工作 30 年，才可以在台北地區買得起一間小公寓。我會試著問孩子幾個問題，你覺得這樣的房價是否合理？為什麼要買房子？如果你有權利能改變些什麼，你要怎麼處理高房價的問題？雖然總會有學生說出那要更努力賺錢的答案，但我想透過討論，孩子可以體認所謂的居住正義是「住者適其屋」的概念，也就是每個人都有適合居住的房子，讓每個人能自由選擇買屋或租屋，而非背著輿論壓力、父母期待、魯蛇的代名詞而被迫去拚房，成為一生的房奴。

翻攝自：Fly Away Home

Fly Away Home《我想有個家》
文／ Eve Bunting
圖／ Ronald Himler
出版社／ Houghton Mifflin Harcourt (1993)
相關影片賞析／
https://youtu.be/GZjC9dAvWuU
https://youtu.be/89Kq8SDyvfg

台灣有哪些幫助孩子學習的機構或單位呢？

可以參考以下資料，或許您也能為教育盡一份心意：

● 火炬助學－立賢教育基金會

● 育成社會福利基金會

● 家扶基金會

● 雅文兒童聽語文教基金會

● 群園社會福利基金會

● 學學文化創意基金會

● 燃燈基金會

● 聯合國兒童基金會

戰地鐘聲

- The Wall
- Rose Blanche
- Four Feet, Two Sandals

戰地鐘聲

The Wall

爺爺的牆

故事摘要

　　位於華盛頓特區的越戰紀念牆，上面刻滿著五萬八千個士兵的名字，他們都在越戰中犧牲或失蹤了。小男孩和爸爸從遙遠的地方來到這裡，面對像鏡子一樣黑黑亮亮的牆，小男孩看見了爸爸和自己，背後有著幾棵枯樹和浮雲，他們慢慢地尋找著爺爺的名字。

　　一個倖存的殘疾老兵坐在輪椅上若有所思地盯著這些名字，仿佛在思念這些逝去的戰友，一位和小朋友奶奶年紀差不多的老婆婆緊緊抱著和我爺爺年紀差不多的老爺爺拭淚，想必他們的孩子在戰場上來不及和他們道別。

　　牆下擺著花朵和其他各式各樣的東西，美國國旗、舊舊的泰迪熊，還有幾封用小石子壓著的信，還有人留下了一朵垂頭喪氣的玫瑰。牆上有太多的名字，這些名字是按照他們死去的年代排列，爺爺在 1967 年過世，爸爸的手指滑過一排排的名字，小男孩也跟著這麼一起找，牆上的字母一個接著一個，好像一排又一排的士兵，整齊又好看，這是一面有溫度的牆。

爸爸終於哽咽著讀出爺爺的名字，他在爺爺的名字上擦了又擦，好像想把它擦掉似的，但也許爸爸只是想記住這個名字摸起來的感覺。爸爸把小男孩抱起來，讓他也可以摸摸爺爺的名字。爸爸把帶來的紙張蓋在爺爺的名字上，用鉛筆在上面輕輕塗著，紙張漸漸變黑，爺爺的名字就拓印在上面。

這時，另一個爺爺帶著他的孫子來到牆前，這小男孩跟爺爺說：「我們可以去河邊嗎？」爺爺拉起他孫子的手告訴他當然可以，但天氣很冷，你需要扣上你外套上的扣子。Gerber 老師也帶著她的學生們走了過來，學生們手中都拿著美國的旗幟，有個女生大聲地問：「老師說這就是為死去的軍人建造的牆嗎？」Gerber 老師和她的學生們說，牆上的名字代表著逝去的軍人們，但這面牆卻是屬於我們每一個人。

爸爸把小男孩的相片放在爺爺名字下面的草地上，一陣風把相片吹走了，小男孩跑去撿回來把它放在原來的地方，並用些小石子壓著，這時他看見照片裡的自己穿過石頭縫對自己微笑。

　　爸爸把手搭在小男孩的肩上跟他說：「這是個光榮的地方，我
覺得爺爺的名字能刻在牆上，是一件很了不起的事。」但是小男孩
更希望爺爺就在他的身旁，能夠帶著他去河邊玩，提醒他扣上外套
的釦子。

　　爸爸和小男孩帶著拓印著爺爺的紙張走向回家的道路，就像帶
著爺爺回家一樣。

大師觀點 / 不同視角看繪本

《爺爺的牆》一書對戰爭沒有隻字片語的控訴，Eve Bunting 用孩子的視角和言語來觀察和表達越戰紀念碑前的哀思，語調始終平實、沉靜，但整個故事讀起來卻張力十足，所營造出的感傷氣氛更渲染了每一個讀者，透過小孩與大人一起緬懷在戰爭中逝去的爺爺，從中體驗戰爭對生命所帶來難以彌補的傷害，讓讀者學會珍惜自己目前所擁有的幸福。

在翻閱這本繪本時，我們不難發現書中插畫大多以灰暗色調為背景，呈現出戰爭帶給人類心靈留下揮之不去的陰影和痛楚，Eve Bunting 運用自己最擅長的鉛筆勾勒和水彩暈染，豐富了作品本身的內涵，小孩身上的那件紅色外套在一片黯淡的背景中更為醒目，紅色渲染著小孩身上的活力與希望，全書黑黑亮亮的正面大理石碑牆在故事中占滿整個跨頁的兩個畫面，

像一面又黑又亮的鏡子，映照出人們不同的思緒，同時讓人類面牆反省，思索戰爭帶給人類的傷害。

Eve Bunting 在說《爺爺的牆》的故事時，利用近物大、遠物小，近物清楚、遠物模糊的繪畫手法，成功的在畫面上製造了深遠的空間感，她就如同大衛芬奇這電影大師一般，透過運鏡將讀者逐漸拉近那面碑牆，讀者翻開繪本會先從遠處看見一大一小的身影，透過畫面逐漸拉近，牆上的文字越來越清晰，期間坐輪椅的軍人、悲傷的老夫婦及牆腳下的泰迪熊及國旗，Eve Bunting 都讓讀者赤裸裸地暴露在華盛頓特區那片碑牆的感傷氛圍中，讓讀者越來越深切地感受到故事中爸爸的哀傷，也越來越看清戰爭的殘酷，鏡頭特寫到爸爸拓印爺爺的名字那一幕更將讀者已經糾結的心狠狠蹂躪了一番。之後，一對祖孫從牆邊走過，慈祥的爺爺緊握著孫子的手，讓人對失去爺爺的小男孩感到心疼，也揭露出小男孩對素為蒙面的爺爺所生的孺慕之情，另一群女學生跟著 Gerber 老師來到牆前，爸爸此時正背對著人群，在爺爺的名字前若有所思的低著頭，女學生在

問了 Gerber 老師許多問題後離開了，隨著師生的身影漸行漸遠，小男孩看似驚訝地握拳摀著嘴，彷彿從 Gerber 老師的回應中得到了對於戰爭的些許解答，所以他轉向爸爸身邊，陪著爸爸一起面牆默哀。

此時，爸爸摺起拓印有爺爺名字的那張紙放在皮包中，拿出小男孩的照片，畫面又特寫到這對父子的表情，平靜而肅穆，最後他們帶著拓印下來的爺爺名字紙張踏上了回家的道路。這個畫面和第一頁開場畫面是同一個場景，頃刻間，一道陽光從尖碑後方灑落，黑雲散去，宛如鋪上一層撒上金粉的輕紗，尖碑頓時光彩奪目，讓人對未來有無限的想像及憧憬，父子倆也正帶著祖父一起回家。

五萬八千多個名字烙印的這面牆上，每個名字背後隱含著多少生離死別的故事，每一個名字代表著一個家庭的破碎，每一個故事又牽連了多少親人、朋友和摯愛呢？戰爭的殘酷透過爸爸及小男孩對爺爺的思念忠實的呈現在各位讀者的面前。

Vietnam Veterans Memorial in
Washington, D.C.
Photo credit: Ingimage

視像思考 /
理解故事脈絡

Falling Action

Event 2:
An old grandpa hugged an old grandma crying. Maybe they were missing their son.

Event 1:
A man who didn't have legs in a wheelchair stared at the names and said hi to the little boy. He dressed like a soldier.

Exposition

The little boy and his father came to visit to the Vietnam Veterans Memorial in Washington D.C. and found the name of the boy's grandfather.

Plot Diagram **The Wall**

Climax

The father's fingers stopped moving along the wall. He finally found Grandpa's name. The father put paper over the letters and rubbed on it with a pencil.

Falling Action

Event 1:

The little boy saw a grandfather holding a boy's hand by the river. The little boy hoped his grandpa could take him to the river and told him to button his jacket as well.

Event 2:

Miss Gerber brought her students to the wall. She said the names were the names of the dead. But the wall was for all of us.

Event 3:

The father put his kid's picture on the grass below Grandpa's name.

Resolution

The Vietnam Veterans Memorial honors the men and women of the armed forces of the United States who served in the Vietnam War. The father said he was proud that Grandpa's name was on the wall, but the little boy would rather have his grandpa here.

批判思考 / 讀出弦外之音

The book did not give much information about the Vietnam War, but what did you learn about the war from the words and pictures in the book?

《爺爺的牆》一書並沒有提及許多關於越南戰爭的資訊，但你又是如何從繪本中的文字及圖片得知戰爭呢？

We don't see any denouncement about the war in the book, but Eve Bunting uses the dialogue between a father and a son to tell the readers the sadness the war brings to us. In the book, we can find most of the pictures' background is grey, which leaves readers an image of sorrow and gloom about the war. People stand in front of the wall to recollect their beloved, while the wall reflects different people's emotions like a black and shiny mirror. The black huge mirror draws every reader back to the jungles of Vietnam in 1960s to see what a real war is. In front of the wall, the father recalled his father by copying an inscription of his father's name. I believe there must be thousands of words he wants to talk to his father.

我們在《爺爺的牆》中並沒有看到隻字對於戰爭的控訴，但 Eve Bunting 用一對父子的對話來告訴讀者們戰爭帶給我們的悲傷。在書中，大部分的插畫以灰暗色調為背景，這也留給讀者們對於戰爭的悲痛與沮喪形象。人們站在碑牆前追憶他們的摯愛；然而這面牆卻如同一面又黑又亮的鏡子反映人們不同的情緒。這面大黑鏡將各位讀者拉回 1960 年代的越南叢林，讓人們看見真實戰爭的樣貌。在牆前的父親用拓印他爸爸名字的方式作為追憶，逸群老師相信此時的他一定有千言萬語想跟他的爸爸說。

2 **You can't see the faces of the boy and his father as they walk away from the wall, but how do you think they are feeling?**

你沒辦法看見爸爸和小男孩的表情當他們離開碑牆時，你覺得他們的心情是如何？

Although we can't see the faces of the boy and his father, we know they must feel relieved. Actually, the scene in the last page is the same as the scene in page 1, but right now, a golden light shines Washington Monument. The sun illuminates the park. The boy and his father are walking toward the light with Grandpa's name in the wallet, which represents they're going to have a bright future with Grandpa's blessing.

雖然我們看不到小男孩和爸爸的表情，但我們知道此時的他們必定覺得很寬慰。事實上，第一頁和最後一頁的場景就是同一個場景。但在此時，一道金色黃光已灑在華盛頓紀念碑上，太陽更照亮了整個園區。小男孩和爸爸帶著錢包裡爺爺的名字走向光明，這也代表著他們帶著爺爺的祝福邁向光明的未來。

教學活動

　　座落於台北市南海路及泉州街交會口的二二八國家紀念館，有兩面牆讓逸群老師備受震撼，一面是「受難者之牆」，另一面則是按原樣複製的「施儒珍之牆」。拿受難者之牆和爺爺的牆相比較，受難者之牆顯示殺戮的殘酷與廣泛，爺爺的牆則是揭露戰爭的傷痛和悲哀，兩面牆上每個名字背後更代表著許多生離死別的故事。在受難者之牆旁還有一座受難者檔案高塔，參觀者可按照姓氏尋找其檔案材料，每一檔案與紀載都讓我不忍卒讀，對那大時代的悲哀感到哀痛。

　　施儒珍之牆堪稱台灣版的安妮的密室，施儒珍是一名深受日治時代文化協會啟蒙運動影響的知識青年，他在二二八時期因參與反對政府的地下組織而遭緝捕，擅長水泥工的胞弟在新竹香山柴屋的牆壁內，另隔出一道假牆，留下二公尺寬的躲藏空間，每日拆磚送飯，以相思樹燒的灰燼混合水泥封牆，在牆壁後側的空間裡，他住了十七年。

　　親愛的老師和家長們，何不找個週末帶上您的孩子去二二八國家紀念館中走一趟，讓我們透過這兩面具時代意義的牆，帶領孩子走回時光隧道，體認台灣今日的民主與自由是多麼的可貴，我們現在所擁有的和平與繁榮是前人用無數血汗換取而來的，讓我們在此默哀一分鐘向那些在二二八事件中的死難者致敬。

翻攝自：The Wall

The Wall《爺爺的牆》
文／ Eve Bunting
圖／ Ronald Himler
出版社／ Houghton Mifflin Harcourt (1990)
相關影片賞析／
https://youtu.be/evepYuiVWjY
https://youtu.be/KztP7SKe0uk

戰地鐘聲

Rose Blanche

鐵絲網上的小花

故事摘要

鐵絲網上的小花這故事發生在二戰時期的德國，有一位名叫 Rose Blanche(蘿絲 · 白蘭琪)的小女孩住在德國的一個小城鎮，原本平靜的生活，因為一群戴著鮮紅色卐字臂章的士兵進駐而改變了，一輛輛的軍用卡車及坦克呼嘯而過，在鵝卵石頭路上濺起無情的火花，機械的聲響震耳欲聾，柴油的味道也讓人須掩住鼻子才能呼吸。

有一天，帶著紅色蝴蝶結髮帶的 Rose Blanche 看到一部因故障停在馬路旁的軍用卡車，車上有一位猶太小男孩跳下來試圖要逃跑，卻被帶著紅色納粹臂章的鎮長擋了下來，他捉住小男孩的衣領把他拎回車上，鎮長沒有多說什麼，只是向納粹士兵嶄露一抹詭異的微笑，那天的天空是灰暗的。Blanche 想知道這個小男孩會被載往何處，於是她跟著卡車一直走，一直走，走進森林中的步道，直到通電的鐵絲網阻擋了 Blanche 繼續向前，鐵絲網後有一排又一排的木屋，一些瘦骨如柴的孩子站在屋前說著肚子餓，Blanche 小心地將麵包遞過去讓他們充飢，盡管是寒冬，這些小孩身上都只穿著一件藍條紋的薄衣，衣服上有顆金黃的六芒星。

幾個禮拜經過了，Blanche 的胃口嚇壞了她媽媽，她袋子裡裝滿了好多的食物去上學，她偷偷的將麵包送給關在鐵絲網後的小孩，Blanche 越來越瘦，但鎮長卻是越來越胖。當雪開始融化，街上開始變得泥濘時，每晚都有軍車不開燈地從河的那一邊開過來，此時的納粹士兵正疲憊的坐在坦克上。

有天，城裡的居民忙著搬離，一批批受傷的納粹士兵也開始離開這小鎮，Blanche 依然帶著麵包進到森林，滿目瘡痍的林地中，木屋不見了，那些在鐵絲網後的孩子也不見了，Blanche 手上拿著一朵紫色小花，神情肅穆地將花朵放在鐵絲網上，煙霧迷漫的光影中隱約看見一些人影，突然一聲槍響劃破了這片寂靜。

鎮上來了另一批的士兵，他們穿的是蘇聯紅軍的制服，但軍車一樣冒出難聞的柴油味，整個鎮上斷垣殘壁，Blanche 媽媽一直在

等小女兒回家，但她大概是等不到了，原本破敗不堪的林地中已被
生機蓬勃的綠地覆蓋，鐵絲網還在，但掛在鐵絲網上的紫色小花卻
已枯萎，而那醒目的番紅花就開在 Blanche 那時所站的地方。

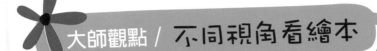

大師觀點 / 不同視角看繪本

　　《鐵絲網上的小花》故事中主角是一個名叫 Rose Blanche（蘿絲・白蘭琪）的小女孩，Rose Blanche 在法語中是一朵白色的玫瑰花，白玫瑰象徵著純潔無瑕的性格以及高貴的人品。

　　在納粹統治期間，有一個知名的秘密組織叫做 Die Weiße Rose，就是德語的白玫瑰，慕尼黑大學的許多學生和教授都是「白玫瑰」的秘密組織中的成員，他們主要對當時的元首希特勒發動侵略戰爭，血腥屠殺猶太人的種種謬行，提出針貶，同時也拯救受納粹迫害的猶太人，後來組織在 1943 年被納粹破獲，同年全部被送上斷頭台，壯烈犧牲。義大利插畫家英諾桑提（Roberto Innocenti）用 Rose Blanche 這個象徵白玫瑰的小人物故事來講述那個大時代的悲哀，其原意就是要彰顯白玫瑰組織無懼死亡，堅守人性美好純良的動人故事，在戰爭、集中營和大屠殺的黑暗中，我們更能看見白玫瑰的純真與善良。

　　英諾桑提在繪製《鐵絲網上的小花》繪本故事時，書中圖畫並沒有出現任何血腥殺戮的場景，但他卻用間接的手法清晰地傳遞戰爭帶給人們的苦難，翻開繪本第一幅畫印入眼簾的是一大群的納粹黨衛軍及那鮮紅的卐字旗，鎮上的居民歡欣鼓舞地向納粹的黨衛軍揮手以表歡迎，Rose Blanche 此時也拿著納粹的卐字旗微笑揮手，歡迎軍隊的到來，畢竟德軍帶給德國人從一戰戰敗後就失去已久的驕傲，鮮紅的蝴蝶結與紅色的納粹卐字旗在這幅畫中特別顯眼，但蝴蝶結與卐字旗的寓意卻截然相反，納粹的旗幟在戰後被視為是猶太人大屠殺的標誌，在德國，法律更明文禁止使用納粹卐字旗，違反的人將會以煽動種族仇恨的罪名起訴，而 Blanche 頭上的蝴蝶結則隱含著純潔、天真和善良的寓意，讀者在翻閱這本繪本時，你會發現帶著紅色蝴蝶結的 Blanche 幾乎都出現在每一幅畫作中，但在 Blanche 最後一次出門給集中營的猶太人送食物時，她卻忘了帶上宛如她附身符的紅色蝴蝶結，這也暗示著純潔善良的 Blanche 將會有所不測，果然一聲槍響劃破這煙霧瀰漫的荒原，Blanche 死了，但在她生前所駐足過的土地上，如今

蒼翠一片，蓊鬱盎然，那朵像蝴蝶結一樣鮮紅的番紅花就開在 Blanche 倒下的地方。春天在歌唱，善良純真的美德重回人間。Rose Blanche 拒絕當一個旁觀者，她的純潔善良及不求回報的善行融化了冰雪，讓我們在這段悲慘沉痛的歷史中看見一絲的光明。

在二戰期間，德國納粹興建了無數的集中營，藉以囚禁猶太人、吉普賽人、同性戀、政治犯及戰俘等數以千萬計的囚犯。奧斯威辛集中營是二戰期間最大的集中營，1940 至 1945 年間，共有 110 萬人在這被處決，其中至少有 100 萬名猶太人。對這些猶太人而言，奧斯威辛集中營不只是工作的場所，更是死亡的煉獄，每日都有無數計的人遭受酷刑、槍決、毒氣等殺害身亡，日以繼夜運作的焚化爐都無法負荷毒氣室中死亡的速度，在奧斯威辛，不論天氣多麼晴朗，天空看起來都是灰的，焚化爐燃燒的灰爐讓天空下的雨更顯汙濁，連呼吸的每一口空氣都是如此沉重。集中營的入口掛著著名的德文標語「ARBEIT MACHT FREI」，意即勞動帶來自由。事實上，這根本就是個謊言，沒有人因為勞動而能夠活著離開奧斯威辛，猶太人終其一生都被勞役虐待，沒有勞動能力者就被直接送往毒氣室殺害，鐵絲網後面是一排又一排的紅磚屋，一式一樣，規律而冰冷，散發著

絕望的氣息。在 1945 年 1 月 27 日，奧斯威辛集中營被蘇聯解放，包括 130 名兒童在內共 7 千名倖存者獲救，每年的 1 月 27 日也被聯合國定為「國際大屠殺紀念日」。

英諾桑提在講述這故事時，刻意用穿著條紋衣服，掛著六角星星，來描述猶太人，用穿著不同制服的軍隊來說明蘇聯的反攻，這樣的刻意就是希望別在讀者心中種下那偏見的種子，人類不該再有種族的標籤與歧視。英諾桑提在最後選擇象徵生命花朵的凋謝呈現 Blanche 的犧牲，不用血腥殺戮的場景，更能感動每一位讀者。面對這段悲痛的歷史，如今我們依舊能感受這道歷史的傷痕，那段人生如螻蟻，道義被踐踏，人性被戕害的過往，我們得銘記於心，身處在台灣的我們，也會明白自己是多麼幸運未曾經歷戰爭的殘酷肆虐。

視像思考 /
理解故事脈絡

Falling Action

Event 3:
Out of curiosity, Blanche followed the truck. She passed the edge of the town, and went into the forest. Everything was frozen.

Event 2:
Blanche saw a Jewish boy jump from the back of the truck. He tried to run away, but the mayor grabbed him and brought him back to the truck.

Event 1:
Blanche's mother warned her to be careful crossing the street because the soldiers wouldn't slow down.

Exposition

Rose Blanche lived in a small town in Germany. World War II erupted. German tanks drove into the town, making sparks on the cobblestones.

Climax

Electric barbed wire stopped Blanche. Behind the wire were hungry Jewish kids. They all wore striped pajamas with a bright yellow star.

Plot Diagram
Rose Blanche

Event 1: Blanche took all the bread she could carry to the concentration camp.

Falling Action

Event 2:

German soldiers started to retreat, Blanche still walked into the forest, but she couldn't find those Jewish kids anymore. She stood still.

Resolution

A shot broke the silence. At that moment in town, Soviet army entered the town. However, Blanche would no longer come back.

批判思考 / 讀出弦外之音

1 The book starts off with Rose Blanche telling the story from a first person point of view. However, about half way through, the author tells the story in the third person. What was significant about this change?

這本書的開始作者用 Blanche 第一人稱的角度去述說這個故事。然而，在故事的中半段卻改用第三人稱敘說故事，這改變有什麼意義呢？

At the start, Rose Blanche didn't understand about the war and the Nazis. She felt like a normal child in a normal German town. To her, the soldiers and the trucks were just an interesting distraction from normal life. She was simply going about her life as a little girl would. However, when she witnessed a boy being taken away by the soldiers, she realized the severity of the war and she was curious why a boy similar to her was being taken away. Upon discovering children who were at the same age of her get in the terrible conditions of a concentration camp, she realized the horrors of war and could empathize with them. So that is the reason the narrator switched from first to third person to underline her changing attitude to the War and the soldiers' occupation.

在故事的開始，其實 Rose Blanche 並不了解戰爭和納粹，她就像一個在德國小鎮上的正常小孩，對她而言，軍人和卡車只是在正常生活中以外一個有趣的消遣，她簡單地過著一個小女生會有的生活。然而，當她

親眼目睹一個小男孩被納粹軍人帶走，她才了解到戰爭的嚴厲，她也好奇地想知道為什麼一個像她一樣的男孩會這樣被帶走。當 Blanche 發現那些和她同年紀的孩子在集中營中的慘狀，她才開始理解戰爭所帶來的恐懼，更同情起這群孩子，這也是為何作者從第一人稱角度出發，在故事中卻轉換成第三人稱的原因，強調著 Blanche 對於戰爭及軍事占領態度的改變。

2

The author, Roberto Innocenti, makes several references to the weather as the story progresses, using it as a metaphor. How is this done? In what ways do you see weather as a metaphor for things that happen or the way you feel?

作者 Roberto Innocenti 在故事進展的過程中提及了許多天氣狀況，並用天氣作為隱喻，作者是怎麼做隱喻的呢？身為讀者，你是否看得出來天氣隱喻著事情的變化及代表的涵意呢？

If you read the text carefully, a lot of weather conditions can be found in the story. It's not hard to find that the weather actually symbolizes a change in atmosphere because of the war. The coming of the winter shows a coming of the war and the despair and bleakness it will bring. Besides, the transformation of the sky to grey and its constant mention throughout the book represents the greyness of normal life experienced by ordinary Germans during wartime. The sky and the river mirror each over. The upper side reflects the real life of Blanche; while the lower side is the reflection of Rose Blanche in the river. You can find that there is barbed wire fence trapping Blanche inside. Actually the author gives the reader a hint that Blanche lives in a world where German are unaware of the concentration camp. The description of the frozen land also represents the children in the concentration camp having their lives frozen behind the barbed wire of the concentration camp. The setting sun describes the impending extinguishing of their lives in the gas chamber. The melting of the snow and the coming of the spring symbolizes rebirth and the ending of the war. The singing of spring also represents the ending of the horrors of war and new life beginning from the misery.

如果你認真地看文本，許多天氣的條件可以在故事當中被找到，讀者應該不難發現天氣的狀況事實上象徵著因戰爭而改變的氛圍，在第一頁中的冬天降臨暗示著戰爭的開端以及戰爭所帶來的絕望和淒涼。此外，書中不斷被提及的灰暗天空更代表著德國人民戰時的灰暗日常，天空和河流互相照映，畫面的上方投影著 Blanche 的現實生活，畫面的下方則是 Rose Blanche 在河中的倒影，讀者可以發現有道鐵絲網籬笆正將河中的 Blanche 倒影困在裡面，其實作者正暗示著讀者 Blanche 正住在一個德國人並未察覺有集中營存在的世界之中，關於冰凍土地的描述也代表著集中營的孩子們在鐵絲網後面所擁有著戰慄的人生，落日則描述著孩子即將在毒氣室中逝去的生命。融雪及春天的到來象徵著重生和戰爭的結束，春天的歌唱更代表著恐懼的結束和悲慘生活中新生命的開始。

3 **After discovering the people behind the barbed wire, Rose Blanche began to sneak food to them. Why did she do so? Why did she keep this secret from her mother?**

在發現鐵絲網後的人們後，Rose Blanche 開始為他們偷偷夾帶食物，為什麼 Rose Blanche 要這麼做呢？為什麼她又要保守這個秘密不給她媽媽知道呢？

I think Rose Blanche must know those people were Jewish kids, and she was educated that Jew were inferior to Germanic peoples. She was told to treat Jewish kids badly. But thanks to Rose Blanche's innocence and kind-heart, she felt sympathetic to their situation. Therefore, she started to sneak food for them without being noticed. That's why she was getting thinner, but at the same time, the mayor was staying fat. Moreover, she needed to keep this secret from her mother because if her mother had known her plan, her mother would have forbidden Blanche to go out again. After all, helping Jew would be executed at that time. Her mother won't allow Blanche to make the big risk.

逸群老師認為 Rose Blanche 一定知道在鐵絲網後的這些人是猶太小朋友，而她所受的教育也告訴著她猶太人比日耳曼民族低賤，她被告知不要善待猶太的孩童，但由於 Rose Blanche 的純真及好心腸，她非常同情這些猶太孩童的處境。因此，她開始為他們偷偷夾帶食物，這也就是為什麼她變得越來越瘦，但同時鎮長卻依舊肥胖。此外，Blanche 需要保守這個秘密，因為如果她媽媽知道了她的計畫，她媽媽或許會禁止她外出。畢竟，在當時幫助猶太人是會被處死的，她媽媽也不會允許 Blanche 冒這麼大的風險。

教學活動

　　在猶太人大屠殺期間納粹使用一個黃色的大衛星來標誌猶太人，它是一個由兩個等邊三角形交叉重疊組成的六芒星形，在猶太教會堂和猶太人的墓碑上都可以看到，從 1941 年 9 月 6 日開始在所有德國占領區內 6 歲以上的猶太人必須配帶黃色的大衛星，中間寫有 Jude（德語：猶太人）的袖章。

　　在逸群老師的繪本課上，我也會做類似這樣的大衛星袖章，讓各組猜拳的輸家別在胸前，那堂課的前十分鐘，我會開始剝奪胸前佩有黃色大衛星孩子的基本權利，他們必須站在教室的後方上課，可以的話我還會準備網子將他們隔開，讓他們有如置身集中營的錯覺，不讓他們喝水、交談、他們還必須做一些勞動服務來換取生存的空間。

　　十分鐘後，我讓這些孩子回到座位，試問他們置身集中營中的感受，以及為何是他們必須被送至集中營被勞役與虐待？種族的標籤與歧視又是否讓我們失去原本的純良。孩子此刻多半靜默，孩子正用他們純潔良善的心去體會那個年代的悲苦。

翻攝自：Rose Blanche

Rose Blanche《鐵絲網上的小花》
文／ Roberto Innocenti; Christophe Gallaz
圖／ Roberto Innocenti
出版社／ Chronicle Books Llc (1990)
相關影片賞析／
https://youtu.be/9ypMp0s5Hiw
https://youtu.be/JdRGC-w9syA

延伸閱讀書單：

● 《穿條紋衣的男孩》（皇冠出版）

● 《夜：納粹集中營回憶錄》（左岸文化）

● 《奧許維茲臥底報告》（衛城出版）

Hitler named German Chancellor

1933
1.30

Germany invades Denmark & Norway

1940
4.9

Germany invades Holland, Belgium and Luxemburg

1940
5.10

Germany invades France

1940
5.13

1933　1939　1940

1939
9.1

1939
9.3

1940
5.10

Germany invades Poland

Britain & France declare war on Germany

Winston Churchill named Prime Minster of Britain

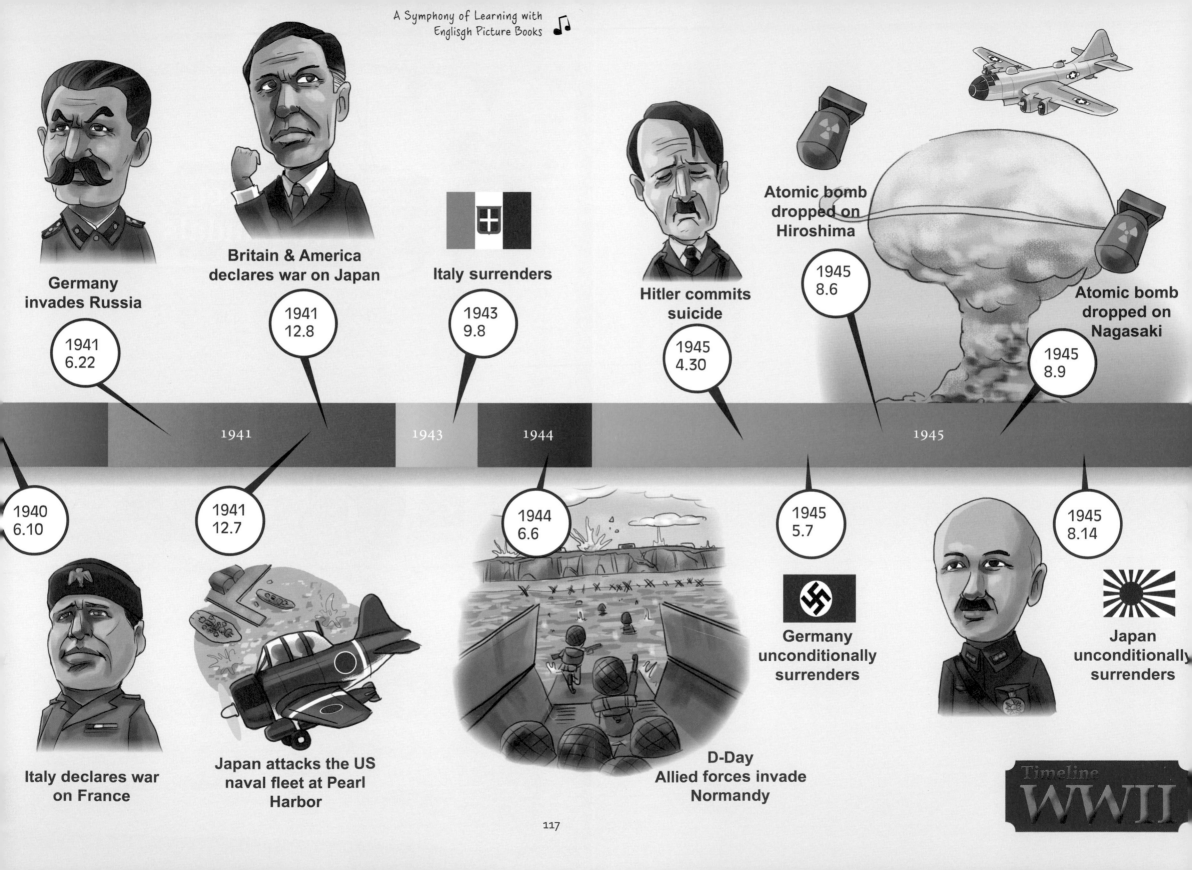

Germany
invades Russia

Britain & America
declares war on Japan

Italy surrenders

Hitler commits
suicide

Atomic bomb
dropped on
Hiroshima

Atomic bomb
dropped on
Nagasaki

1941
6.22

1941
12.8

1943
9.8

1945
4.30

1945
8.6

1945
8.9

1940
6.10

1941
12.7

1944
6.6

1945
5.7

1945
8.14

1941 1943 1944 1945

Italy declares war
on France

Japan attacks the US
naval fleet at Pearl
Harbor

D-Day
Allied forces invade
Normandy

Germany
unconditionally
surrenders

Japan
unconditionally
surrenders

Timeline
WWII

117

戰地鐘聲

Four Feet, Two Sandals

四隻腳，兩隻鞋

故事摘要

　　兩個互不相識的阿富汗女孩，因為戰爭的緣故和家人逃到巴基斯坦邊境的難民營。在一次發放救援物資時，所有人蜂擁而出，緊緊抓住自己搶到的東西，十歲大的 Lina 搶到了一隻合腳的全新涼鞋，她開心極了，因為她已經兩年沒有穿過鞋了，她趕緊尋找另一隻鞋子，但卻發現鞋子的另一腳被另一個女孩撿走，她叫 Feroza，而她的腳乾踵得像塊饅頭。很快的 Lina 和 Feroza 在河邊相遇，各自穿著一隻夢想已久的鞋子，她倆決定湊成一雙輪流穿以解決「四隻腳，兩隻鞋」的困境。

　　隨著日子過去，Lina 和 Feroza 一起在河邊洗衣，一起排隊取水，沒事做時他們躲在學校的窗外偷聽老師上課，以木頭為筆，在沙地上練習寫著自己的姓名，一日早晨，傳來了 Lina 的名字出現在安置家庭名單上的好消息，她將從難民營離開前往美國展開新生活。故事最後，離別之際的兩人決定各自保留一隻鞋子，以此紀念他們在這苦難歲月下的友誼，這雙鞋讓 Lina 和 Feroza 邂逅了彼此，也讓她們在戰爭的烽火下產生了患難扶持的友誼。

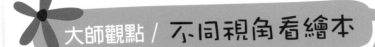

大師觀點 / 不同視角看繪本

　　《四隻腳，兩雙鞋》的故事是作者 Karen Williams 依照卡卓拉 (Khadra) 在柏夏瓦難民營 (Peshawar refugee camp) 的經歷真人真事改編而成，柏夏瓦是個介於阿富汗和巴基斯坦邊境的城市，由於阿富汗長年處於戰亂不穩定中，迫使數百萬的阿富汗人必須逃離家園，遠走鄰國，許多難民就在柏夏瓦附近搭建臨時營帳，形成一個規模龐大的柏夏瓦難民營。

　　Karen Williams 在寫《四隻腳，兩雙鞋》的故事時，全世界有超過兩千萬名的難民每天活在不確定與恐懼之中，且大多數的難民都是孩童，雖然這故事是根據卡卓拉的真人真事改編而成，但 Lina 和 Feroza 這兩個小女生所經歷的苦難卻是世界各地難民的共同經驗，相信許多難民此時也期待著跨越邊境來到歐洲或美國展開新的人生，為家人找到一個安全

的避風港。

　　近年來的歐洲移民危機，要從 2010 年 12 月 17 日北非的突尼西亞的警察因取締一名無照販售水果的失業大學生說起，水果攤販因此憤而自焚，這消息也透過社群網站快速傳播，讓原已居高不下的失業率和高漲糧價的民怨更深，進而導致一連串的警民抗爭，並擴大為反政府與爭取自由民主的浪潮，媒體將此次事件稱為「茉莉花革命」，以突尼西亞的國花茉莉花命名。

　　2011 年春季開始，受茉莉花革命成功的影響，六個阿拉伯國家的人民起義推翻獨裁政府，樂觀地把「一個新中東即將誕生」預見為這個運動的前景，也就是人們熟知的「阿拉伯之春」。然而，突尼西亞的成功卻只是整個區域裡微弱的光點而已，其他的五個國家都沒能因革命而換來快樂的結局，利比亞淪為軍閥內戰的動亂國家，葉門成為沙烏地阿拉伯和伊朗的代理人戰爭的戰場，巴林則變得更加的保守和專制，埃及雖曾迎來短暫的民主時光，但新政府執政經驗的缺乏，一連串失敗的伊斯蘭化的施政及重回威權的傾向，埃及人民再度走上街頭，

只是這次對抗的卻是經由民主大選選出來的政府，抗爭帶來的動亂使得軍方有理由以穩定之名行奪權之實，五年過去，埃及重回革命前的原點。

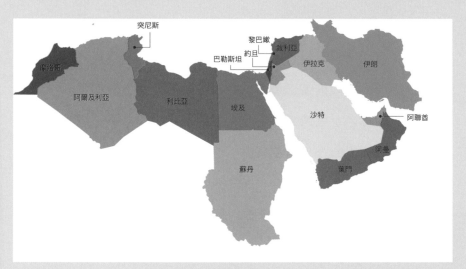

最鮮明的失敗例子非敘利亞莫屬，敘利亞自古處在亞州中心，是絲路綠洲貿易路線的中繼點，多民族、教派、文化的融合成就大馬士革的繁華，如今的敘利亞已經淪為一個生靈塗炭的內戰國家，伊斯蘭國崛起，國家瀕臨毀滅，這五個國家不是更加獨裁，便是墜入內戰的深淵，阿拉伯之春如今已是破碎的美夢。來自中東、非洲和亞洲的大人帶著小孩，不斷冒險搭乘皮筏或超載的船隻，試圖跨越地中海或經由巴爾幹半島進入歐盟國家尋求居留，人類的苦難、生命的韌性與希望，以及被拒絕入境

的景象也一再上演。這是一個 21 世紀的出埃及記，中東的難

民遷徙到歐洲平均一個人需要花費 2,200 歐元，折合台幣大約

是 80,000 元，一家人必須要賣掉房子、珠寶、汽車只為了一

個安全的棲身之處，途中還得躲避警察的盤查，划著橡皮船橫

越浩大的地中海。然而，對這些飽受戰火摧殘的難民來說，能

夠找到個不用畏懼砲火、戰事、殺戮，一個可以安心路眠的地

方，那地方對他們而言就是天堂，可那永遠不是家鄉。

Photo credit:　Azzam Daaboul

世界各地的難民每天都活在不確定與恐懼之中，《四隻腳，兩

隻鞋》的繪者 Karen Williams 以一個以友情為基底，發生在

難民營中的故事，告訴著我們這些現深受苦難的難民所擁有的

力量、勇氣和希望。

視像思考／
理解故事脈絡

Lina raced barefoot to the refugee camp entrance where relief workers threw used clothing off the back of a truck. Lina squatted down and grabbed a sandal.

Each girl wore a sandal to the stream and met each other They decided to take turns wearing the sandals.

One morning, Lina's name was on the resettlement list. Lina and her mother were flying to America. Lina's mother bought her leather shoes for America, so she decided to leave the sandals for Feroza.

Four Feet, Two Sandals
Based on a true story

Feroza, who was thinner and darker than Lina, wore the other blue and yellow sandal.

Lina

Feroza

Feroza handed Lina one sandal. "What good is one sandal?" Feroza said, "It's good to remember." Perhaps they would share the sandals again in America.

批判思考 / 讀出弦外之音

1 What do the sandals represent to Lina and Feroza? (p10)

這雙涼鞋對 Lina 和 Feroza 而言代表著什麼呢？

The sandals here represent the friendship between Lina and Feroza. At the beginning of the story, Lina and Feroza owned a single sandal. But it was inconvenient to wear only one sandal, so they decided to share the sandals, one day each. We know that sharing is the true essence of friendship. When Feroza knew that Lina was on the resettlement list, she bent down and took the sandals off. Feroza handed the sandals to Lina and said, "You cannot go barefoot to America." The sandals here represent the great blessing from a great friend. In the end, they decided to keep one in order to remember the hardship they had endured in the refugee camp. Besides which, each sandal is also a pledge that they would meet again.

這雙涼鞋象徵著 Lina 和 Feroza 所擁有的友誼。故事的一開始，兩個小女生各擁有一隻涼鞋，但只穿一隻鞋走路卻是相當不方便的，於是他們決定每天輪流穿這雙涼鞋，我們知道分享才是友誼的真諦，在當 Feroza 得知 Lina 在安置名單上時，她彎下腰將涼鞋脫下要送給 Lina，她說：「你不能光腳去到美國。」這雙涼鞋在此象徵著一個好朋友的祝福。最後兩個女生決定各自保留一隻涼鞋以紀念他們在難民營中的苦難歲月，此外，她們所各自擁有的涼鞋也變成了她們再次相見的信物。

2 What is the European refugee crisis? What impact has it caused on Europe?

歐洲的難民危機是什麼呢？難民危機又帶給歐洲什麼樣的衝擊呢？

The European refugee crisis began in 2015, when a rising number of refugees and migrants made the journey to the European Union in order to seek asylum. They needed to travel across the Mediterranean Sea or through Southeast Europe. Syrians, Afghanis and Iraqis are the top 3 nationalities that compose the majority of refugees. Europe is experiencing the highest influx of refugees since World War II. The refugee crisis has also caused some social problems for European countries, such as public security issues, loss of job opportunities and a reduction in local's living standards. Tensions in the EU have been rising because of the disproportionate burden faced by some countries, particularly the countries which have open borders and provide shelter for refugees, like Greece, Italy and Hungary.

歐洲的難民危機爆發於 2015 年，大量的難民和移民開始往歐盟國家移動尋求一個安全的庇護所，他們必須要橫渡地中海或是穿越南歐才能得到些許的休息，難民人數最多的三個國家為敘利亞、阿富汗和伊拉克。歐洲目前正面臨著二次大戰後最大的難民湧入潮。難民危機也導致不少社會問題，像是治安問題、當地工作機會減少和居住品質的低落。歐盟的壓力也因各國難民收容的分配不均在持續地上升，特別是那些對難民敞開大門並提供庇護的國家，如希臘、義大利和匈牙利。

Do you think Taiwan should allow refugees into our country? Share your opinion.

你認為台灣應該要允許難民進入到我們的國家嗎？和大家分享一下你的想法吧！

Right now, it's a critical moment for the world, and we are writing history as we speak. How do we want to be remembered? As xenophobic, rich cowards hiding behind fences? We have to realize that these people fleeing death and destruction are no different from us. By accepting them into our country and integrating them into our society, we can sustain our aging population. Although some social problems will occur, such as crime and cultural differences, we have much to gain. Don't forget we are proud to say "The most beautiful scenery in Taiwan is people." Our children will learn compassion and empathy. There is something to be lost if we ignore this crisis. More dead children are sure to wash ashore if we don't act with humanity. Let's do this right and try to be the best we possibly can be.

我們的世界正面臨關鍵的時刻，而寫歷史的正是我們。你又想要如後被後人所記住呢？一個躲在圍欄後面的排外有錢懦夫？我們必須了解到這些逃離死亡和戰亂國家的人們跟我們沒有不一樣，藉由接納他們進入台灣並讓難民融入我們的社會也可解決台灣人口老化帶來的相關問題。雖然一些像是文化差異及犯罪的社會問題會產生，但我們會得到更多，我們不都很自豪地說「台灣最美的風景是人。」我們的孩子也將會學會關懷跟同理，我們如果持續忽略難民危機，相信我們會失去更多，會有更多的孩子像敘利亞男孩一樣地死在岸上，讓我們盡力的將人道工作做到最好吧！

教學活動

　　《四隻腳，兩隻鞋》講述兩個難民營中的女孩，因一雙涼鞋而結緣的友情故事。逸群老師在做這本繪本故事教學時，會請孩子們穿拖鞋來上課，接著讓孩子兩兩一組，我會拿著箱子要求一組學生交出一雙拖鞋，並要求孩子們共享一雙拖鞋，讓他們體會故事中兩位女孩四隻腳，兩隻鞋的困境。

　　接著進行「21 世紀的出埃及記」難民體驗遊戲，孩子們須從中東地區出發搭飛機到達土耳其，聚集到港口城市伊茲密爾，而後轉乘偷渡船穿越地中海前往希臘或義大利，搭乘巴士或小客車穿越馬其頓到塞爾維亞，路途中要盡可能的躲避當地警察的盤查，接下來得步行進入匈牙利境內，有些販運集團會將大量的移民塞在狹小的貨車中越過邊境，從東歐的匈牙利移動到中歐和北歐國家，因為路途比較遙遠，要以巴士、計程車和火車轉乘。這些移民大多希望前往德國、瑞典等庇護法規完善的國家，因為這些國家大多提供受庇護的難民基本的生活補助教育資源和物資補給。

　　這趟旅程我會讓孩子兩兩一組，揹著對方並手持道具飛機的方式前往土耳其，過程中腳不能落地，落地代表著在逃難的過程中死亡，我用拖車製作了兩艘偷渡船，讓孩子搭乘穿越地中海前往希臘和義大利，兩台拖車的容量顯然有限，不少孩子在此關卡選擇放棄或腳不小心落地而結束遊戲，只剩下三位孩子成功到達目的地，接著他們必須以「老漢推車」的方式走到教室的盡頭並折返才代表他們能成功抵達中歐。

　　孩子在遊戲中還能感受到樂趣，但難民面對的是真正的逃難，遊戲的結束對他們而言就是生命的結束，而有幸能夠到達目的地的難民，還得面臨著漫長的申請、歧視、工作權等新的挑戰。對走過這一趟新世紀的出埃及記的人們來說，能夠不再畏懼砲火、戰事和殺戮，安心入眠可能就像天堂，但那永遠都不是家鄉。

翻攝自：Four Feet, Two Sandals

Four Feet, Two Sandals《四隻腳，兩隻鞋》

文／ Karen Lynn Williams; Khadra Mohammad

圖／ Doug Chayka

出版社／ Eerdmans Pub Co (2007)

相關影片賞析／

https://youtu.be/uuVRwDBiKws

https://youtu.be/ua5vOJo-34s

性別平權

- Piggybook
- My Princess Boy
- And Tango Makes Three

性別平權

Piggybook

朱家故事

故事摘要

　　Piggott 先生有兩個兒子，Simon 和 Patrick，他們住在很好的房子裡，有很好的花園，還有一輛很好的車子在很好的車庫裡，而在這間屋子裡還有他的妻子。

　　故事一開始，Piggott 先生與他的兩個孩子 Simon 和 Patrick 意氣風發的站在屋子前，要吃早餐時，朱爸爸跟他的孩子們只要嚷嚷著，茶來伸手、飯來張口，在朱爸爸出門上班，朱小弟們出門上學後，媽媽便開始洗碗、鋪床、吸地毯，然後出門上班。

　　傍晚時分，放學跟下班的老爺和公子們回家第一件事情就是嚷嚷著晚餐，媽媽馬上為家中老爺和公子們準備，當他們享受眼前美食時，媽媽卻是在洗碗、洗衣服、燙衣服，然後還得準備自己的晚餐，老爺和公子們這時慵懶地躺在沙發上看著電視。

有一天，朱公子們回到家中卻沒有聽到熟悉的「你們回來啦」，朱爸爸問：「你們的媽媽呢？」原來媽媽留下一張你們是豬的紙條後離家出走了。

　　朱家老爺和公子們瞬間變成了三隻小豬，連家中的時鐘，窗外的月亮及森林的形狀都成了豬的模樣，他們必須花好幾個小時才能做好自己的餐點，而且食物難吃的要命，他們從不洗碗、從不洗衣服，很快的小窩就變成了豬窩，孩子們都在問：「媽媽什麼時候才要回家？」

　　一晚，家中已經沒有存糧，三隻小豬們正在尋找地上的食物碎屑充飢，門打開了，折射出門一樣大的光芒，媽媽的身影彷彿就是聖母瑪利亞的化身。求求你，回來吧！三隻小豬向媽媽跪求著。

　　從這刻開始，Piggott 爸爸開始洗碗、燙衣服，Patrick 和
Simon 也開始自己整理床鋪，一家人一起做美食，這時的朱媽媽心
情愉悅，表情陽光，帶著幸福的微笑，此時的她正在修理家中的汽
車！

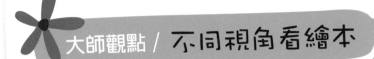

大師觀點 / 不同視角看繪本

　　朱家故事的作者是有「超現實藝術家」美譽的 Anthony Browne，他以超現實的插畫手法及想像力，帶領讀者穿梭於現實與想像之間的一本談論性別平權的繪本，Anthony Browne 擅長在繪本故事的插畫中置入線索，讀者能藉由這些線索讀出故事的弦外之音，讓逸群老師帶大家從這些插畫線索中來探索朱家故事所要教導我們的事情吧！

　　朱家故事的英文標題是 Piggybook，英文裡面有一個和 Piggybook 相似的字就是 Piggyback，Piggyback 有把重物扛在肩上的意思，而封面上神情凝重的媽媽背著開心愉悅的朱爸爸和兩個兒子的圖片值得每個家庭深思，這畫面彷彿是一位任勞任怨的媽媽對一個不做家事的丈夫及兩個不懂感激的孩子的無聲抗議。

　　翻開第一頁，印入眼簾的是朱爸爸與他的孩子們雙手環抱胸前，一副君臨天下的帝王站姿，但我們卻看不到媽媽的身影，Anthony Browne 似乎在一開始就告訴了讀者在朱家，男性主宰一切，這是一個沙豬主義瀰漫的家庭，這也是為什麼作者會將這本書取名叫做 Piggybook，因為標題的 Piggy 不正也暗諷著擁有大男人主義者的沙豬們（Male Chauvinist Pig），中文標題朱家故事中的「朱」更與沙豬的「豬」諧音雙關。

接著我們會看到媽媽辛勤地做著家事的插畫，從凝重抑鬱的色調中，不難推測出此時朱太太的心情可能不太美麗，從畫中朱太太的臉龐也格外模糊，彷彿就如同她在家中的地位一樣輕微，沒有存在感。

　　有天，媽媽終於無法忍受朱家如女傭般的對待，離家出走，家中壁爐上的名畫〈安德魯斯先生與夫人〉，畫中安德魯夫人變成了一片空白，壁爐上的信件就像是變了心的女友給男友的 Dear John letter（分手信），信中的字條寫著你們這群沙豬（You are Pigs.），朱媽媽用最溫柔的震撼爭取自己的尊嚴。

少了媽媽，朱家父子們一瞬間變成了三隻小豬，平常嬌生慣養慣的他們不會做飯、不會洗碗，宛如生活白癡，Anthony Browne 此時將窗外的夜色描繪成有如大野狼的化身，也暗喻著風暴的來襲。

索性這時家中大門打開，一道光線灑在漆黑的家中，地上投射出來的是媽媽如聖母瑪利亞般的倒影，牆上名畫〈笑容騎兵〉中神采飛揚的騎士瞬間變成了大豬頭，爸爸與孩子

們在地板尋找食物碎屑的情境就有如伏地認錯的罪人般，跪求著媽媽的寬恕，在天主教信仰中，聖母瑪利亞代表的是慈悲和寬恕，媽媽此時用慈愛的心寬恕了自己的丈夫和心愛的孩子，此時的朱家少不了媽媽，再也沒有缺陷。

　　故事的最後，朱媽媽表情陽光、面露微笑著修著朱爸爸的愛車，車子在當今社會可說是男人彰顯身份地位的工具，朱爸爸願意將愛車給朱媽媽維修，顯現他已經放下男人的自負，車牌號碼 SGIP 321 也告訴了我們朱媽媽將這三隻小豬（123 PIGS）的大男人主義思維徹底的翻轉，也為朱家故事做了最好的註腳。

You are pigs.

Mrs. Piggott's job

Mrs. Piggott prepared breakfast for his family every morning.

Then, she washed the dishes, made all the beds, vacuumed all the carpets and went to work.

After work, she prepared dinner for her family every evening.

Then, she did the laundry, the ironing, and cooked some food for herself.

Housework Allocation Piggybook

Mr. Piggott's job

Reading the newspaper & eating all the time.

Mrs. Piggott leaves her home.

Mr. Piggott and his sons beg Mrs. Piggott to come back. They promise help with the housework.

Moral

Gender equality is important in a family. Every family member has a responsibility to help with the housework.

批判思考 / 讀出弦外之音

1 **Why did Anthony Browne name this book-"Piggybook"? If you were the mother on the cover, how would you feel? (cover)**

為什麼 Anthony Browne 將此書命名為朱家故事呢？如果你是封面上的媽媽，你的感受又是什麼呢？

When I first saw the cover, I observed the mother is bent over with a heavy burden on her back--- her husband and her two sons. I felt pity for her. Apparently, she takes most of the responsibility for keeping things running in the Piggott family. Her husband and her sons wear big smiles on their faces and do nothing. That may be why Anthony Browne has named this book "Piggybook," because Mr. Piggott and his two sons are just too lazy. After I read the whole story, I found that the Piggott family is a patriarchal family. Men don't have to do any housework at home. "Chauvinist pig" is the perfect term for Mr. Piggott, Simon and Patrick. No wonder this book is called "Piggybook."

當逸群老師第一次看到朱家故事的封面時，只見一位媽媽辛苦地背著她的丈夫及兩位孩子，身兼如此重擔，我都開始同情起她。顯然朱媽媽在家中扮演起一家之主的角色，而朱爸爸與朱小弟們面帶微笑，整天閒閒無代誌，這或許是為什麼 Anthony Browne 將此本繪本命名為朱家故事的原因吧！畢竟朱爸爸和朱小弟們實在是懶得像頭豬了。讀完整本繪本，逸群老師發現朱家根本是一個男性至上的重男輕女家庭，男性在家不用做任何家事，「沙豬」根本就是朱爸爸和朱小弟的專有代名詞。朱家故事完美呈現豬圈的生活。

2 **What is mentioned at the beginning of the story? Did you find anything missing in that paragraph? (p1)**

故事的開頭提到了什麼東西呢？你有發現什麼東西被遺漏了嗎？

Anthony Browne mentions Mr. Piggott and his two sons, Simon and Patrick at the beginning of the story. They were standing with their arms crossed in front of the house, like an emperor with his sons. Some other material considerations are also mentioned, like the nice house, the nice garden, the nice car and the nice garage. But it's only at the very last that he mentions his wife (who's inside the house). Why is Mrs. Piggott not nice? Or she is just an accessory to the Piggott family? By the end of the story, you will have discovered all the answers.

故事開頭出場的是朱爸爸和朱公子們，他們雙手環抱胸前，以君臨天下的帝王之姿站在屋前，而文字接著帶到許多物質的東西，如一間好的房子，一片好的花園，一台好車及一個好的車庫，最後才提到房屋裡還住了他的老婆。而且「好」字似乎在這邊被遺漏了，朱媽媽是真的不好嗎？還是她就只是朱家老爺們的附屬品呢？在讀完這本書後，你就會知道所有的答案。

3 **Why is everything in the story in the shape of a pig? Which one is your favorite?**

為什麼故事中的許多東西是以豬的形狀出現呢？你最喜歡的圖片又是哪一張呢？

As the story develops, more and more pig images appear in the story. Maybe it's because Anthony Browne is trying to imply to readers that this is the process of how Mr. Piggott and his two sons became pigs. So eventually you can even see how Mr. Piggott and his two sons really become pigs on page 16. However, my favorite picture is on page 19. Their expressions are so panicked and helpless. Outside the house a big bad wolf is howling. Faced with this situation, Simon and Patrick look to their father for help. Apparently, his father can't do anything. Fortunately, Mrs. Piggott comes back as the image of the Holy Mother. Mr. Piggott and his sons kneel down in front of Mrs. Piggott and ask for redemption. This picture left a big impact on me.

隨著故事的進展，讀者們可以發現越來越多豬的形象出現在故事中，或許 Anthony Browne 試圖在暗示讀者 Piggott 先生和他兩位公子正在成為豬的過程，你會發現在故事的 16 頁，朱爸爸和朱公子們終於真正的變成三隻小豬。然而，逸群老師最喜歡的圖畫是 19 頁中朱小弟仰望著他們的爸爸，眼神驚慌無助地希望爸爸找出辦法，面對外頭嘶吼的大野狼，爸爸卻也只能回報驚慌無助的眼神，幸運的是，朱媽媽這時以聖母的形象回到家中，畫面中朱爸爸與朱公子們跪在地上彷彿在尋求救贖般地渴求媽媽的原諒，這真的是一張令我非常印象深刻的圖片。

④ What does Piggybook say about gender equality? What's your opinion about gender equality?

朱家故事如何說性別平權這件事情？說說你對性別平權的看法？

Mr. Piggott and his two sons behave like pigs towards poor Mrs. Piggott. Finally, she walks out. Left to fend for themselves, the male Piggotts undergo some curious changes. They start to share some housework which was previously a woman's task. Conversely, Mrs. Piggott starts to fix the car which belongs to Mr. Piggott. Nowadays, cars usually represent the power and status of a man.

Therefore, it's a great improvement in gender equality that Mr. Piggott allows a woman to fix his car. The story also suggests to readers that everyone should share the housework in a family--- no matter if you are a man or a woman. In my opinion, everyone should receive equal treatment and not be discriminated against based on their gender. And of course, that includes transgender people as well, who should be respect based on who they are.

朱爸爸和朱小弟們在家的行為就像是頭大懶豬，朱媽媽受不了這樣的待遇終於離家出走，朱公子們被迫得自謀生計，他們終於有了難以置信的改變，朱家公子們開始分擔以前屬於女性的家事。相反地，朱媽媽卻開始修理屬於朱爸爸的名車，車子在今日通常是一個彰顯男人身分與地位的工具，所以我們可以從朱爸爸允許一個朱媽媽來修理他的名車的情況看來，顯然性別平權的概念在朱家有很大的進步，朱家故事也告訴讀者們每一個家庭成員不論性別都應該分擔家務。逸群老師覺得每個人都應該被平等的對待，不會因為自己的性別而遭到歧視，即使是第三性，我們都應該對他們的選擇予以尊重。

教學活動

　　在進行《朱家故事》的繪本教學時，老師或家長可以問問孩子目前家中的家事都是如何分工的呢？家中的家事又是否是媽媽一個人的責任？逸群老師在課堂中會進行朱家故事的角色扮演遊戲，請孩子四人一組，一位扮演朱爸爸，一位扮演朱媽媽，兩位扮演朱小弟，並讓扮演朱爸爸和朱小弟的孩子帶上豬鼻子道具，此時，我會開始發號司令，四點一到，請朱小弟們拿起手機呼叫朱媽媽來學校接他們回家。五點鐘，則是朱小弟的點心時間，朱小弟們又得要求朱媽媽準備他們心愛的點心來填飽肚子。六點鐘，朱媽媽得開始準備晚餐。同時，朱爸爸正拖著疲憊的身軀返回家中，朱爸爸嚷嚷著要朱媽媽幫他準備洗澡水，好讓他從緊繃的壓力中放鬆一下。七點鐘，全家開始享用朱媽媽用心準備的晚餐，在電視機前，邊看新聞邊吃著飯的朱爸爸想吃些水果，又呼喊著朱媽媽削上他最喜歡的蘋果。晚餐過後的八點，朱媽媽還得洗碗。九點鐘，收拾朱家一家人的衣物準備開始洗衣服、曬衣服，十點鐘，還得檢查朱小弟的功課是否完成，簽完聯絡簿後的朱媽媽已經累的不成人形。試問問扮演朱媽媽的孩子內心的感受，同時我們再回到課堂開始時的那個問題，家中的家事是否是媽媽一個人的責任呢？我想答案已經在孩子的心中。

翻攝自：Piggybook

Piggybook《朱家故事》
文／ Anthony Browne
圖／ Anthony Browne
出版社／ Dragonfly (1990)
相關影片賞析／
https://youtu.be/rD7VoYtBkVM
https://youtu.be/5Ja1AKJeko4

性別平權

My Princess Boy

我的公主男孩

故事摘要

　　我的公主男孩是一個四歲的小男孩，他喜歡穿粉紅色的洋裝，他跳起舞來就像芭蕾舞者一樣的優雅。他喜歡芭蕾舞的旋轉，他喜歡在爬樹時帶著他的公主男孩皇冠。在購物時，他會選最閃亮的洋裝和小女生的首飾。生日派對上，他大方表示：「我是個公主男孩」來歡迎來派對的公主朋友們。萬聖節時，他更直接打扮成一個公主和他哥哥去要糖果，他是我的孩子，Dyson。

　　有些人會取笑我的公主男孩，但我不會。當他在買粉紅色包包或閃亮亮衣服時，人們用詭異地眼神盯著他，有些人不只取笑他，也取笑身為媽媽的我，這讓我們都很受傷。我會跟我的公主男孩說，當他穿上裙子時有多麼漂亮，我的公主男孩可以穿著女孩的衣服和我玩耍，他的爸媽都愛著他，他的爸爸會拉起他的小手，給他一個如公主般的旋轉，我的公主男孩也會和爸爸要抱抱。他還有一個很酷的哥哥，他哥哥喜歡棒球和足球，而且他哥哥和我的公主男孩會一起跳舞。

　　但如果你碰到了一個公主男孩，你會取笑他嗎？你會污辱他嗎？還是你會和他一起玩？你會不會喜歡他原本的樣子？

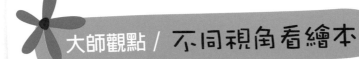

大師觀點 / 不同視角看繪本

　　《我的公主男孩》以一個媽媽的角度出發，用媽媽的口吻呼籲讀者們一起學習接納，以勇氣和真誠道出自己身為一個跨性別者的媽媽，看見孩子在社會上所遇見的問題。這是一本談無條件的愛、社會接納和家庭支持的繪本，更呼籲著社會接納多元，停止任何形式的性別批判與霸凌。

　　跨性別這個詞英文為 transgender，trans- 來自拉丁文，有「超越、跨越、在另一邊」的意思，gender 則是指性別，簡而言之，跨性別是指「性別認同」與「出生時被指定的性別」不同的人，《我的公主男孩》中的 Dyson 即為一位跨性別的小男孩。而跨性別者往往承受著自己性別認同與社會期待相異、性別刻板印象以及法律規定等的壓力，故事中的 Dyson 就因為想買粉紅色包包及閃亮亮洋裝遭到他人的異樣眼光和訕

笑。在現實生活中，跨性別孩童甚至連上廁所都有可能產生問題。其實，跨性別者在智能、社交及生活能力上與一般人並沒有差異，Dyson 有個愛他的爸媽和哥哥及一群幫他慶生的好朋友，但他的內心深處是否正面臨著家庭、學校與社會上的歧視與壓迫呢？這些自我的心理壓抑，讓身為 Dyson 媽媽的 Cheryl Kilodavis 以感性口吻來呼籲讀者一起來愛這位公主男孩原本的樣子。

不知道在閱讀《我的公主男孩》時，你有沒有發現裡面的角色都沒有臉孔呢？逸群老師猜想，作者可能是希望讀者能夠將自己投射進不同的角色，設身處地思考跨性別者的困境，這本暖色系粉紅底的繪本呈現了一個媽媽如何從徬徨、困惑、心碎到接受的心路歷程。

視像思考/
理解故事脈絡

Series of Events Chain
My Princess Boy

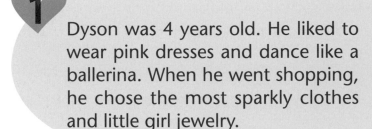

1

Dyson was 4 years old. He liked to wear pink dresses and dance like a ballerina. When he went shopping, he chose the most sparkly clothes and little girl jewelry.

2

For Halloween, Dyson dressed like a princess. At his birthday party, he greeted everyone by announcing "I am a Princess Boy!" and waved his wand.

3 Somebody laughed at him because he was in a princess dress. But his mom and dad loved him just the way he was, and his brother celebrated his uniqueness.

4 His mother, the narrator, asked the reader not to laugh and call him names, but to accept him for who he was.

5 With courage and honesty, Dyson's mother addresses a social taboo-transgender identity. The mother asks for acceptance with judgement and support for all children no matter how they wish to look.

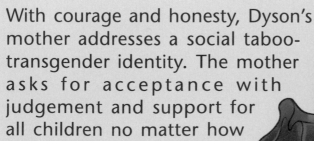

批判思考 / **讀出弦外之音**

1 **Why do you think author Cheryl Kilodavis decided to write "My Princess Boy"? What do you think she hopes to accomplish by writing this book?**

為什麼作者 Cheryl Kilodavis 決定要寫《我的公主男孩》呢？
你覺得她希望藉由寫這本書實現什麼呢？

Cheryl Kilodavis had a four-year-old son. He liked to play dress up with girly dresses and was laughed at when he wore them to school. As a Princess Boy's mother, she got hurt. She feared that her son would be teased or bullied in the school. Based on this experience, she introduced the difficult themes of diversity, being different, being unique and bullying to the readers. At the end, powerful questions are directed to at the readers for to think about and discuss: "If you see a Princess Boy....Will you call him a name?...Will you like him for who he is?" She hopes everyone can learn to accept the difference and respect the diversity. With empathy, we can appreciate the uniqueness of others. It is because of the uniqueness that Princess Boy can be that special. Compassion takes effort. It takes focus. It takes commitment. It takes practice."

Cheryl Kilodavis 有一個四歲的孩子，他喜歡穿著女生的洋裝，但也因為這樣他會被別人取笑。身為一個公主男孩的媽媽，她是很受傷的，她更害怕她的孩子在學校被戲弄和欺負。基於這樣的經驗，她將多元、差異、獨特、霸凌的議題介紹給讀者們。在故事的最後，許多提供讀者思

考與討論的問題被提了出來：「如果你遇見了一個公主男孩，你會汙辱他嗎？還是你會喜歡他原本的樣子？」她希望每個人能夠學習接受差異和尊重多元。有著同理心，我們才能夠欣賞別人的獨特，也是因為這樣的獨特性，公主男孩才能這樣的特別。憐憫需要經過努力，它需要被聚焦，它需要承諾，它也需要被練習。

 Why does the illustrator chose not to put faces on the figures in the book?

為什麼插畫家選擇把角色用無臉的方式呈現呢？

The illustrations in the book show faces with no features, presumably to remind readers that the characters could be anyone. The walnut-shaped faces don't allow readers to judge the characters' emotions from their facial expression, which also forces them to search inside themselves, aiding the cognitive processes of empathy. Besides, if you only see the illustrations, you can't judge the character's gender. After reading the text, you will find the main character is a boy; even though the character is wearing a skirt. This kind of gender shock challenges the reader's gender identity. It can help readers to learn the beauty of being unique.

書中所有插畫的臉部都沒有任何的特徵表情，作者大概是希望提醒讀者，這些角色可能是你身邊的任何人，這些胡桃形狀的臉，讓讀者無法從他們的臉部表情判斷出這些角色的情緒，這也強迫讀者們去探究自己的內在，有助於同理認知歷程的養成。此外，如果你只看插畫的話，你根本無法辨別出這個角色的性別。在讀完文本後，你會發現主角是個小男孩，即使他穿著裙子。這樣的性別衝擊挑戰讀者的性別認知，幫助讀者去學習看見獨特的美。

3 Ultimately, Princess Boy is happy because he is loved for who he is by his family and his friends. What is unconditional love? How does your family show you unconditional love?

公主男孩最後因為家人及朋友的關愛而得到開心，這是種無條件的愛。什麼是無條件的愛呢？你的家人又如何對你展現無條件的愛呢？

Unconditional love is a kind of affection without any limitations; it is a love without conditions. It's a type of love which has no boundaries. Unconditional love is frequently used to describe love between family members, comrades in arms and between others in highly committed relationships. When I was in junior high school, I had quarrels with my mom very often. Because of my immaturity, my mom often cried late at night. But my mom always forgave me no matter how unreasonable I was. She took care of me when I was sick. She gave me a ride to the school and cooked delicious meals for me. Right now, it's my turn to take care of her in return. I love you, Mom.

無條件的愛是一種沒有任何條件限制的愛，一種沒有邊界的愛。無條件的愛經常被使用在形容親人、共患難的戰友或是有忠貞關係的彼此上。在逸群老師國中時期，我常常與媽媽發生爭吵。也因為我的幼稚，媽媽時常在夜深人靜時哭泣，但無論我如何的不講理，媽媽總是會原諒我。她在我生病時照顧我，她載我去上學，煮好吃的東西給我吃。現在該是我回報她的時候了，讓我照顧你。媽媽，我愛你。

教學活動

　　《我的公主男孩》這本以媽媽口吻談論跨性別議題的繪本是否有引起讀者你的共鳴呢？建議老師或家長們在進行此繪本教學前，可準備一件裙子，尋求自願的男生穿上在校園生活一整天，記錄下你與他人互動的感受，受到什麼樣的對待，又有沒有被取笑或是揶揄呢？看著這孩子的紀錄，試想想如果你是這男孩的媽媽，你會不會徬徨與困惑？你又想不想保護你的孩子呢？試想想此時這男孩心中的感受，或許他正躲在一角因你的揶揄而暗自哭泣。逸群老師經常在課堂中安排教學體驗活動，讓孩子親身去體驗那種被貼標籤或被歧視的感受，無非是希望透過這些親身感受，能讓孩子體會被霸凌者的痛楚，藉此學習接納與包容，人與人有太多的差異，如何學習尊重多元，欣賞個別的差異和學會同理他人，是我最希望帶給孩子們最珍貴的一堂課。

翻攝自：My Princess Boy

My Princess Boy《我的公主男孩》
文／ Cheryl Kilodavis
圖／ Suzanne Desimone
出版社／ Aladdin Paperbacks (2010)
相關影片賞析／
https://youtu.be/LB_2-gsH8GE
https://youtu.be/d88APYIGkjk

性別平權

And Tango Makes Three

一家三口

故事摘要

　　《一家三口》描述一個紐約中央公園動物園中的真實愛情故事，故事主角是一對雄性南極企鵝：Roy 和 Silo。他們彼此相愛就如同其他企鵝伴侶一般生活、相愛，他們向彼此鞠躬、一起散步、一起高歌、一起游泳，無論 Roy 去哪，Silo 都陪在他的身旁。

　　在企鵝孵蛋時期，他們卻面臨了他們想做卻不可能做到的事情，他們看到其他企鵝媽媽生下小企鵝蛋，企鵝爸爸與媽媽輪流孵蛋的樣子，他們也好想跟他們一樣，但他們生不出企鵝蛋，他們也沒有企鵝寶寶可以餵、可以抱抱、可以苛護。於是 Roy 找到了一顆和企鵝蛋很像的小石頭，Silo 開始細心的照料和孵化，但終究無法如其他伴侶般孵育出小企鵝。

　　動物園內的保育員 Gramzay 先生發現了此現象，此時另一對企鵝家庭 Porkey 和 Betty 生下了兩顆企鵝蛋，由於南極企鵝的習性只會照顧其中一顆企鵝蛋，Gramzay 先生就決定將沒人照料的那顆企鵝蛋放到 Roy 和 Silo 的巢中，成就他們想與其他企鵝伴侶一般的孵育歷程。

　　有天，蛋殼內傳來呱呱呱的叫聲，企鵝寶寶從裂蛋中躦了出來，Gramzay 決定將企鵝寶寶命名為 Tango(探戈)，因為探戈需要兩隻企鵝才有辦法一起跳，而 Tango 也成為中央公園動物園中第一隻擁有兩個爸爸的企鵝寶寶。

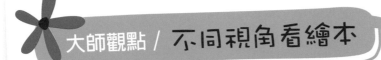

大師觀點 / 不同視角看繪本

　　《一家三口》改編自紐約中央公園動物園的真實愛情故事，它從一段動物的情誼讓我們看到生物真實的多元樣貌，作者 Justin Richardson 和 Peter Parnell 本身就是一對同志伴侶，且透過代理孕母生下他們的女兒，親身的經歷與繪本故事中的企鵝生活相互連結，在「動物、人類、故事、現實」的關係中更有著許多密不可分的呼應與對話。

　　《一家三口》是 And Tango Makes Three 的中文譯名，其中 Tango (探戈) 一字源於英文諺語 It takes two to tango，這句諺語直譯是要兩個人才有辦法跳探戈，也可以寫成 It takes two to make a quarrel，譯為兩個人才有辦法吵架，引申意思為有爭議時雙方都必須負責任，通常用來暗示吵架時雙方都有錯，中文也有類似諺語「一個巴掌拍不響」。探戈據說取源於情人之間的祕密舞蹈，所以在古代男士在跳探戈時都佩帶短刀，舞者表情嚴肅，表現出東張西望，提防被人發現的神情，探戈更有挺拔俊俏、倜儻灑脫、剛勁有力的風格。

　　繪本故事中的 Tango 是一對同志伴侶 Roy 和 Silo 的小孩，其中隱含著愛如同探戈般需要有更多的突破與解放的意思，讀者也必須將原本只限於兩人組合的探戈解放，才能明白企鵝家庭中一家三口的真諦，愛是組成家庭中最重要的元素，而從這本繪本故事中我們也得知了愛有許多不同的可能性。

　　目前台灣教育體系中的性別教育多半都還停留在性別刻板印象的探究階段，但我們的社會卻已開始對性別認同、多元性別取向、同性婚姻、多元成家的議題產生對話。《一家三口》透過動物間的愛情故事讓我們反思性別差異，也讓性別平權的議題向下扎根，讓我們的孩子在求學階段就能接觸性別平權的相關議題，一本書能夠改變一個人的價值觀，也能打開一個人的世界觀，如何以平常心，不帶偏見的觀點來閱讀此本繪本，並看待自然界的各種現象，認識世界的寬廣不就是一個閱讀引領者的使命嗎？

And Tang

視像思考／
理解故事脈絡

1 Roy and Silo were male penguins living in the penguin house in Central Park Zoo. They were a little bit different from other penguins.

3 Their zookeeper, Gramzay, noticed that Roy and Silo had fallen in love with each other.

5 Mr. Gramzay found an egg that needed to be cared for, and he brought it to Roy and Silo's nest.

Roy

Makes Three

2 They bowed to each other, walked together, sang to each other, and swam together. Wherever Roy went, Silo went, too.

4 Roy and Silo wanted to have a baby chick to feed, cuddle and love, but it was impossible for them to have a baby. Therefore, Roy found a rock which they could hatch. They took turns keeping the rock warm. But nothing happened.

6 Squawk, squawk, peep, peep. Tango was born. Tango became the very first penguin in the zoo to have two daddies.

Silo

批判思考 / 讀出弦外之音

① **How did Mr. Gramzay know Roy and Silo were in love? How did Mr. Gramzay help Roy and Silo to form a family? (p9)**

Gramzay 先生是如何發現 Roy 和 Silo 墜入愛河呢？他又是如何幫助 Roy 和 Silo 組成一個家庭的呢？

Although Roy and Silo were both boys, they did everything together. For example, they bowed to each other, walked together, sang to each other, and swam together. Wherever Roy went, Silo went, too. Both male penguins didn't spend much time with the female penguins. Instead, they wound their necks around each other. Those intimate actions revealed that Roy and Silo fell in love with each other. They have been a couple since 1998. As a zoo keeper, Mr. Gramzay even gave Roy and Silo a chance to become a family. In 2000, another penguin couple named Betty and Porkey laid two eggs. They couldn't take care for more than one egg at a time. Therefore, Mr. Gramzay decided to bring one egg to Roy and Silo's nest. Roy and Silo took turn hatching the egg. Their baby was born with everyone's blessing. If you go to the Central Park Zoo, you can see their kid, Tango splashing with his friends in the penguin house. There are forty two chinstrap penguins in the Central Park Zoo and over ten million chinstraps in the world. But there is only one Tango.

雖然 Roy 和 Silo 兩個都是男性，但他們做什麼事情都在一起。舉例來說，他們彼此鞠躬，一起散步，一起高歌，一起游泳，無論 Roy 去哪裡，Silo 一定緊跟著他。兩隻男性企鵝沒有花太多的時間在女性企鵝身上；相反地，他們頸部環繞著彼此的頸部，這些親密的行為顯示著 Roy 和 Silo 兩人墜入了愛河。事實上，他們從 1998 年就是一對情侶了，身為動物保育員的 Gramzy 先生甚至給 Roy 和 Silo 一個機會組成家庭。在 2000 年時，另一對企鵝情侶 Porkey 和 Betty 生下了兩顆企鵝蛋，但他們沒有辦法同時照顧兩顆企鵝蛋，因此，Gramzy 先生決定把其中的一顆蛋帶到 Roy 和 Silo 的巢中，Roy 和 Silo 開始輪流孵化這顆蛋，他們的小孩也在眾人的祝福下出生。如果你有機會到訪中央公園動物園，你會看到他們的孩子 Tango 正在和他的企鵝朋友們潑水，在紐約的中央公園動物園有 42 隻的南極企鵝，世界上也有超過一千萬隻的南極企鵝，但 Tango 卻是獨一無二的。

 2 **What do all families have in common? Do you find it in Roy and Silo's family?**

所有的家庭都有什麼共通元素呢？你可以發現這元素在 Roy 和 Silo 的家庭當中嗎？

Love is the common element in every family. You can find the love element when Roy and Silo got along with each other. They took care of each other. They were just like other penguins. They desired to have their own baby. At first, Roy found a rock for Silo to hatch on it. But it was impossible for them to have a baby under this circumstance. One day, Mr. Gramzay finally brought one egg to Roy and Silo's nest. They did their best to take care of this egg. They moved the egg to the center of their nest. Every day they turned it, so each side stayed warm. Some days Roy sat while Silo went for food. Other days it was Silo's turn to take care of their egg. Their baby came out under their care. Roy and Silo became fathers, and Tango was their kid. This family was composed of love, just like other family. 故事愛是每個家庭所擁有的共同元素，你可以在 Roy 和 Silo 的相處中發現愛的元素，他們照顧彼此，他們就和其他企鵝一樣，他們也渴望擁有自己的小孩。起初，Roy 找了顆石頭讓 Silo 可以在上面孵化小北鼻，但這明顯行不通。有一天，Gramzay 先生終於帶了一顆蛋到 Roy 和 Silo 的巢中，他們盡全力來照顧這顆企鵝蛋，他們把企鵝蛋移到巢中央，每天都會翻動這顆蛋，讓每面都保持溫暖，有些日子 Roy 在孵蛋，Silo 出外覓食；有些時候換到 Silo 來照顧他們的寶貝蛋，他們的小北鼻在他們的細心照料下出生，而 Roy 和 Silo 雙雙成為了父親，Tango 也成為他們的小孩，這個家庭由愛所組成，就跟你我的家庭一樣。

3 Do you think whether gay marriage should be legalized?

你認為同性戀婚姻應該被合法化嗎？

Marriage is a keystone of our social order. No union is more profound than marriage, for it embodies the highest ideals of love, fidelity, devotion, sacrifice, and family. There is no difference between same or opposite-sex couples with respect to this principle. Heterosexual couples can get married when they are in love. Same-sex couples should have the equal right. They should also have the right heterosexual couples have when they get married, like legitimate right of inheritance, health benefit and income tax. In front of love, everyone is equal. They are no different from us. Everyone has the freedom to love and the right to pursue happiness.

逸群老師認為婚姻是人類社會秩序的基石,沒有一種結合比婚姻制度來的更深刻,因為婚姻體現了愛情、忠貞、犧牲和家庭的最高典範。同性伴侶和異性伴侶在面對這婚姻的準則上並沒有不同,異性伴侶在相愛時可以走入婚姻,同性伴侶也應該擁有相同的權利,他們應該擁有異性戀伴侶結婚所擁有的權力,像是法律繼承權、醫療及賦稅上的保障權,在愛之前,大家都是平等的,他們和我們並沒有不同,每個人都該有自由去愛和追求幸福的權利。

教學活動

台灣同志遊（Taiwan LGBT Pride）是每年十月底在台北市會舉辦的活動，吸引台灣各位社會運動者及同志團體的參與，主要目的為提供一個公開現身的平台，凝聚志同道合者的力量喚起社會大眾注意，讓隱藏的問題曝光、末見的需求被重視，進而建立更多元包容的社會及價值。

遊行當天彩虹旗海飄揚，隊伍浩浩蕩蕩的出發，但也有反同志團體高聲呼喊維護家庭價值，堅持一男一女，一夫一妻的婚姻制度。不知道老師或家長們有沒有和孩子探討同性婚姻是否該合法化的議題呢？逸群老師在上《一家三口》的繪本故事前，會先請孩子上網搜尋婚姻平權議題相關資料，進行辯論，藉由辯論，孩子能夠交換彼此想法，在說服別人的過程中，也同時檢視了自己的價值觀，讓我們展開對話，而非攻訐，用不帶偏見的角度來詮釋這本性別平權繪本。

翻攝自：And Tango Makes Three

And Tango Makes Three《一家三口》
文／ Justin Richardson; Peter Parnell
圖／ Henry Cole
出版社／ Simon & Schuster (2005)
相關影片賞析／
https://youtu.be/zt2w1NdQZ2E
https://youtu.be/5vvq87M03qk

延伸閱讀書單：

- Mommy, Mama, and Me
- Daddy, Papa, and Me
- Stella Brings the Family
- Heather Has Two Mommies

夢想驛站

- Miss Rumphius
- The Tree Lady
- With Books and Bricks How Booker T. Washington Built a School

夢想驛站

Miss Rumphius

花婆婆

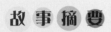

　　《花婆婆》這本繪本透過一個小女孩來講述花婆婆的生命故事。遲暮之年的花婆婆是小女孩的姨婆，她告訴她的姪女說，很久以前，她還是個小女孩，名叫 Alice。Alice 的爺爺開了一間藝品店，晚上，Alice 常坐在她爺爺的腿上聽她講遠方的故事，Alice 心生嚮往，她告訴爺爺，等長大以後她也想向爺爺一樣到遠方旅行，當她老了，也要像爺爺一樣住海邊，爺爺笑著請 Alice 長大以後一定要記得做一件讓世界更美麗的事。

　　很快的，那個年輕的 Alice 長大了，大家改叫她 Miss Rumphius（盧小姐），她離開家鄉來到一個離海很遠的城市，作一個圖書館員，幫大家找到他們想要看的書並且也看了很多的書，都是關於很遠的地方所發生的故事。接著她開始四處旅行，她去熱帶島嶼，島上的人養猴子和鸚鵡當寵物，盧小姐還爬過高大的雪山、穿過熱帶叢林、橫越沙漠，看過獅子嬉戲和袋鼠跳。最後她來到東方的一個小國，在那裡，她從駱駝背上摔了下來，背部因此受傷了，盧小姐自責自己的笨手笨腳，但也因此開啓她要做的第二件事，到海邊找個房子住下來。

定居海邊的花婆婆生活幸福美滿，但她常常望著大海，思索著要做什麼事情才能讓這世界更美麗。有一天，當她踏上山頂，望著一大片藍色、紫色、粉紅色的魯冰花時，她想到了一個很棒的點子。從那天，她每次散步時就會隨手撒下魯冰花的種子。隔年春天，那些種子都開花了！原野上、山坡上開滿了藍色、紫色、粉紅色的魯冰花，魯冰花沿著公路和鄉間小路盛開著，連空地上和高聳的石牆下也都開滿著美麗的魯冰花。花婆婆終於完成了她答應爺爺的三件事，現在的花婆婆像她爺爺一樣，正在跟圍在她身旁的小朋友們說著遠方的故事。

小女孩告訴花婆婆，等她長大後，也要像花婆婆一樣去很遠的地方旅行。當她老了，也要像花婆婆一樣住在海邊，並且做一件讓世界變得更美麗的事。

大師觀點 / 不同視角看繪本

　　仔細品嘗《花婆婆》這本繪本，逸群老師發現花婆婆的故事不只是一本簡單談及夢想的繪本，其中還包含了花婆婆與爺爺濃厚的祖孫情誼，兒時的花婆婆常坐在爺爺的腿上聽她講遠方的故事，爺爺也告訴花婆婆一定要做一件讓世界更美麗的事情，長大後的花婆婆同樣告訴她身邊的孩子們一定要讓這世界更美麗，這種美好生命的感染力無形的在祖孫之間傳承下去，也讓我們知道環保、愛地球、讓世界更美麗這些事情不只是一個人要做的事情，而是要代代相傳的不斷傳承。

　　《花婆婆》的作者 Barbara Cooney 在這本繪本中以感性的口吻講一個生命故事來喚醒人們心目中的那個夢想，這個夢想並非是遙不可及的夢想，花婆婆帶給讀者的是希望，她播下的每顆種子更是大家希望的種子，不知道讀者們有沒有發現故事的開頭與結尾的插圖，爺爺講故事給花婆婆聽時所在的客廳壁畫和花婆婆講故事給孩子們聽時所在的客廳壁畫是相同的兩幅畫，Barbara 用圖畫告訴了讀者花婆婆與爺爺的生命感染力著實在祖孫之間傳承下去，其中一幅畫畫著汪洋中的一條船在

暴風雨中的乘風破浪，這也告訴我們完成夢想的過程從來不是簡單的，需要歷經很多的苦難和努力，另一幅的熱帶小島告訴了我們夢想成真後的美麗果實是如此美麗，最後花婆婆也對讀者們提出了一個邀請，「如何做一件讓世界更美麗的事情？」邀請讀者除了完成自己的夢想，也要讓這個世界因你的夢想而變得更加美好。

五月天的歌曲「頑固」，講著交通大學教授吳宗信教授在 20 年前放棄在國外發光發熱的機會，回到台灣只為一圓在台灣製作火箭並發射至太空的夢想，在 2012 年他與秉持著相同太空夢的 40 個師生籌建了 ARRC（前瞻火箭研究中心），不斷嘗試火箭試射實驗，誓言研究出探空火箭。

在我們的社會中，其實也有許多像花婆婆一樣的人，做著讓這個世界變得更美好的事。可是看在一般人眼裡，或許也像故事書中那些鄉民一樣，認定她是「怪婆婆」，我們常常為了自己而忙碌，忽略了這世界上仍有許多值得你付出的人事物，逸群老師要跟大家分享其實要讓世界變得更美麗，並不是要做什麼了不起的大事。只要一個小小的行動和滿滿的愛就可以達成這個夢想，手心向下是助人，主動向身旁的人伸出溫暖的雙

手，隨時以微笑示人，彼此分享生活中的喜樂，互相幫助，用真心來看待每件人事物，我相信這個世界將會更美麗、更快樂、更溫暖，讓我們都成為一顆愛的種子，並將這良善的種子傳承下去吧！

視像思考 /
理解故事脈絡

Mis

Grandpa

Do something to make the world more beautiful

2

Miss Rumphius walked on the long beaches, picking up beautiful shells in a real tropical island, where people kept cockatoos and monkeys as pets.

The next spring, there were lupines everywhere. Miss Rumphius had done the third, the most difficult thing of all: making the world more beautiful.

Miss Rumphius

Rumphius

1

Alice moved to another city far from the sea and the salt air. She worked in a library, dusted the books and kept the books from getting mixed up, and helped people find the ones they wanted. Some of the books told her about faraway places.

Alice

One day, Miss Rumphius got off a camel. Her back hurt.

3

Miss Rumphius remembered there was still one thing she needed to do. She started to sow lupines by scattering seeds along the highway and along the country lanes.

Lupine Lady

批判思考 / 讀出弦外之音

1 **What three things did Alice promise to do for her grandfather? Do you think Miss Rumphius really accomplished them? (p6)**

Alice 答應爺爺做哪三件事情？你覺得花婆婆有做到她答應她爺爺的這三件事情嗎？

When Alice was a little girl, she set two goals for herself. She would follow in her grandfather's footsteps by traveling to faraway places and then settle down in a home by the sea. Alice's grandfather tells her there is one more thing she must do. She must do something to make the world more beautiful. Alice agrees to honor her grandfather's request, but she doesn't know how she will do it yet. After Alice grows up, she accomplishes her goals of traveling around the world and finding a home by the sea. Still, Miss Rumphius wonders how she will make the world more beautiful. Then one spring day, after having spent many months in bed with a bad back, Miss Rumphius discovers that the lupines she had planted in her garden had spread to a nearby hill. Miss Rumphius orders five bushels of lupine seed and begins to sow them wherever she goes that summer. By the next spring lupines are growing all over her seaside town and Miss Rumphius, now known as the Lupine Lady, has accomplished her grandfather's request. The thing Miss Rumphius did probably doesn't mean a lot to you, but everyone smiles upon seeing those lupines blossom all about the town. In addition, Miss Rumphius graciously entertains the neighborhood children with stories of faraway places, and asks them to do something to make the world more beautiful.

當 Alice 是個小女孩時,她為自己設立了兩個目標。她會遵循她爺爺的腳步到許多遙遠的地方旅行並找到一個在海邊的家安頓下來。爺爺告訴她還必須再做一件事情,做一件讓世界變得更美麗的事情。Alice 同意了爺爺的要求,但她還不知道她要做什麼事情讓世界變得更美麗。Alice 長大後,她完成了環遊世界的目標並且找到了一個在海邊的家,但她仍然不知道要做什麼讓世界變得更美麗?在春天的某一天,她因病臥床好幾個月後,花婆婆發現她種在花園的魯冰花已經開滿了整個山丘。於是,花婆婆在夏天無論走到哪兒都開始播種魯冰花。春天來臨時,魯冰花盛開在海邊城鎮的每一個角落,花婆婆,也就是我們知道的魯冰花女士,在此刻已經完成爺爺的三個承諾。花婆婆所做的一切對你我來說可能意義不大,但城鎮中的每一個居民一看到盛開的魯冰花都因此嶄露他們許久不見的笑容。花婆婆也用這些遙遠地方的故事來娛樂這些小朋友們,並且也要求他們要做一件讓世界變得更美好的事情。

2 How do the different names in the story represent the main character? From Alice, Miss Rumphius, Crazy Old Lady to Lupine Lady.

故事中主角的不同名字代表著什麼意涵呢?故事中主角的姓名從愛麗絲、盧菲絲小姐、瘋狂老太婆到魯冰花夫人又意味著什麼呢!

Those names represent Miss Rumphius' life journey. We can see little Alice grow up, mature and become a wise woman by accomplishing her grandfather's requests. Miss Rumphius has different names at each step. The character is named Alice when she is a little girl. Like Alice in Wonderland, Alice is a girl who dreams of traveling to faraway places. She sets out on different adventures and experiences different lives. From Miss Rumphius, Crazy Old Lady to the Lupine Lady, these name changes represent the process of a young girl gaining wisdom over the course of her life. The neighborhood children call her the Lupine Lady, which also shows readers that she has won over the hearts of those children.

這些名字象徵著 Miss Rumphius 的人生旅途，我們可以看見小 Alice 藉由著完成爺爺的要求而蛻變成一個有智慧的夫人，花婆婆在不同的階段擁有不同的姓名，當她小時候時叫做 Alice，就像是愛麗絲夢遊仙境般的 Alice 一樣，她夢想著去遙遠的地方旅行，她歷經不同的冒險並體驗不同的生活，從盧菲絲小姐、瘋狂老太婆到魯冰花夫人這些都代表著這女生得到人生的智慧，這些小朋友稱她一聲魯冰花夫人也告訴了讀者花婆婆贏得了這些小孩們的心。

3 **Miss Rumphius is a story about legacy. Just as Alice was asked by her grandfather and then Alice asked her niece, "what will you do to make the world a more beautiful place?" Now, I'm asking you, "what are you going to do to make the world a more beautiful place?**

花婆婆是一個具有傳承意義的故事。就像是爺爺要求 Alice，花婆婆要求她的姪女承諾做一件讓世界更美麗的事情一樣。現在讓逸群老師問你，你要做什麼事情讓這世界變得更美好？

Recently, I bought a folding bike and started to ride my bike to the school every day. Due to global warming, the Earth's temperature is becoming hotter. Human beings have already caused too much carbon emission. It's time for humans to see the destruction we have caused to the Earth. Riding a bike not only reduces carbon emissions, but also benefits our health. I even established a biking club at our school. We ride our bikes to save our earth and make the world a better place.

逸群老師在最近買了一台小折腳踏車,打算每天騎小折去學校上班。因為全球暖化的關係,我們的地球變得越來越熱,人類已經製造過多的碳排放量,是時候我們該檢視我們人類對地球所做的傷害。騎腳踏車不僅能減少碳排放,還能增進我們的健康,逸群老師甚至在學校創立了單車社團,用騎腳踏車來拯救我們發燒的地球並讓這個世界更美好。

教學活動

　　《花婆婆》教會了我們做一件讓世界更美麗的事情，這件事情不是要驚天地，泣鬼神，夢想再遠大，也要從點滴做起。花婆婆用行動告訴了讀者，隨手撒下的魯冰花種子也能讓世界更美麗，只要你持之以恆的一直做下去。老師或家長可以請孩子想出一件讓世界更美好的事情，持之以恆的做一個月，並用社群媒體忠實紀錄，讓這棵真善美的種子發揮影響力，影響身旁的人，一個月後，讓我們再來回顧這一切，相信老師或家長們都會替這孩子的所作所為感到驕傲。

翻攝自：Miss Rumphius

Miss Rumphius《花婆婆》
文／ Barbara Cooney
圖／ Barbara Cooney
出版社／ Puffin Books (1985)
相關影片賞析／
https://youtu.be/_pCtXRP1edo
https://youtu.be/YKiMrg6rgYQ

寫下你立願的夢想清單：

夢想驛站

The Tree Lady

樹媽媽

故事摘要

　　Katherine 生長於美國加州北部的森林中，她從小喜歡收集像樹和榆樹的樹葉，她也喜歡收集松針和紅木針，她會用花朵裝飾，將這些樹葉和針葉編織成美麗的項鍊和手鍊。在 1860 年代，在 Kate 居住的城鎮中，沒有一個孩子的雙手是髒兮兮的，但 Kate 除外。

　　上學以後，大多數的女孩不喜歡科學研究，但 Kate 不同，她對自然界的風和雨、人體的肌肉和骨骼、植物和樹木特別感興趣。大樹對 Kate 而言就像是巨大的雨傘，是萬物生靈的守護者，不是所有人都覺得森林是他們的歸宿，但 Kate 除外。長大後的 Kate 選擇進入大學攻讀科學，並成為加州大學理學院的唯一女性畢業生。

　　畢業後，她來到南加州州的學校教書，並身兼該校的副校長，當她搭的船停靠在聖地牙哥時，她發現她來到了荒無人煙的沙漠小鎮，那裡幾乎一棵樹都沒有。從她的教室裡，Kate 可以看見在山丘上的城市公園，但城市公園一點都不像是個公園，那只不過是一個人們放牛吃草和傾倒垃圾的地方。聖地牙哥人不相信在乾燥的土地

上能夠生長出大樹，Kate 例外。她辭掉工作，成為一個辛勤的園丁，

她寫信給全世界的園丁，請他們寄來不同種類的樹木種子。

由於她的努力，1915 年，巴拿馬—加州博覽會正式在改名為貝

爾波爾公園（Balboa Park）的場地舉辦，Kate 知道公園內還需要

更多的樹木，她的事蹟感動了城市裡的許多居民，他們紛紛自願前

來種樹。開幕當天，五湖四海的賓客齊聚一堂，他們在 Kate 種的樹

下乘涼，他們都無法相信聖地牙哥有這樣

壯麗的花園。1940 那年，Kate 辭世，人

們稱她為貝爾波爾公園的母親，她從事種

樹的志業直到生命的最後一刻。在過去，

沒有人能想像聖地牙哥能夠成為一個綠意

盎然的城市，Katherine Olivia Sessions

做到了，憑著一步一腳印，她成為這個城

市最偉大的園藝師。

Balboa Park
Photo credit: Ingimage

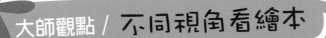

大師觀點 / 不同視角看繪本

《樹媽媽》的作者 H. Joseph Hopkins 在造訪南加州後，深深地被這座城市的都市樣貌所產生的反差而著迷，在南加州有著荒蕪的沙漠，卻又有蓊鬱盎然的貝爾波爾公園，當他發現原來 Katherine Sessions 這位樹媽媽是這座城市花園的推手後，他開始用筆記錄樹媽媽的生命故事。這本賦有開拓和環保精神的繪本，講述樹媽媽 Kate 將一個荒蕪的沙漠之城變成了今日鬱鬱蔥蔥的聖地牙哥，身為綠拇指先鋒和綠色行動主義者的 Kate 用她的生命故事感動每一位讀者，相信 Kate 的善念會在每一位讀者心中生根萌芽。

在閱讀這本繪本時，不知道你有沒有發現作者往往用 But Kate did 做為結語，Kate 也真的做到了許多人做不到的事情，她是一個小女生不怕手髒的與花草為伍，在自然課時總是

要坐在第一排，她能夠在森林中找到平靜，更成為第一位從加州大學理學院畢業的女性，她也是一位在荒蕪城鎮中種出一片森林的樹媽媽，她說服了一群願意像她一樣「傻」的人一起動手種樹，就是這樣的恆心與毅力，她改變了這個城市。

從《花婆婆》到《樹媽媽》，兩位堅持夢想的女性都用自己的方式讓這個世界更加美善，花婆婆用魯冰花點綴鎮上每一條鄉間小路，樹媽媽則是用恆心與毅力靠著種樹改變聖地牙哥原先的荒蕪，從兩本繪本中我們可以看見女性力量（girl power）的強大，這仿佛就是一場溫柔革命，她們用內心的纖細及堅毅的溫柔，憑著自己的雙手一花一草的改變這個世界。

視像思考／
理解故事脈絡

Timelin
The Tree L

Kate became the first female science graduate from California University. After graduation, she took a teaching job in Southern California. She found that her new home was a desert town.

Katherine Olivia Sessions grew up in the woods of Northern California. She got her hands dirty in her childhood. She was interested in studying science. She had a great passion for trees. Trees seemed like giant umbrella sheltering her.

1881

1860s

1915

1883

With Kate's love for the woods, she thought San Diego needed trees more than anything else. So she left teaching to become a gardener. Soon Kate's trees were planted along streets, around schools, and in small parks and plazas all over the town.

The Panama-California Exposition was held in Balboa Park. She asked for volunteers to plant trees together. The fairgoers couldn't believe San Diego had such magnificent gardens. She continued gardening and planting trees until her death. People called her " The Mother of Balboa Park."

批判思考 / 讀出弦外之音

1 In the story, you can read the repetition of the pattern "Not everyone....But Kate did!" nearly every page, why does the author use the pattern repetitively?

在故事中的每一頁，你都可以讀到「不是每個人都……但 Kate 做到了。」這個重複的句子，為什麼作者要重複使用這樣的句子呢？

The author uses repeated lines at the end of each page ("Kate did it") to emphasize Kate's determination to create a beautiful oasis in the desert. Whether it represents the limitations of gender expectations, scientific challenges or career choices, nothing can stop Kate once she makes up her mind. She was a girl who wasn't afraid to get her hands dirty. Most girls were discouraged from studying science, but Kate always sat in the first row during science class. She became the first female science graduate from California University. Those achievements showed how mighty girl power is. With the determination and perseverance, she became a green-thumbed pioneer, and made San Diego a lush, leafy and flourishing city. Kate finally did something others couldn't do.

作者不斷用了「Kate 做到了」來彰顯 Kate 要在沙漠中建造一個美麗綠洲的決心。不管它是否代表著對女性角色的期待、理科的種種挑戰或是職涯選擇的限制，一旦 Kate 下定決心，沒有任何障礙能夠阻止她往夢

想邁進。她是一個不怕手髒髒的女孩。當大多數的女生對研讀科學洩氣時，Kate 在自然課時總是坐在第一排。她也成為第一位從加州大學理學院畢業的女性。這些種種成就都展現「女性力量」的十足強大，藉由著決心和毅力，Kate 成為了綠拇指的先鋒並把聖地牙哥變成了一個都市花園，Kate 終於做到了其他人做不到的事。

What do you learn from Kate Sessions?

你從 Kate Sessions 身上學到什麼呢？

Kate Sessions is a girl who never follows the norm. She is also a dream maker who thinks big but starts small. Her story encourages every girl to study in science. Her story inspires every reader to follow their heart. Her story teaches children that they can be whoever they want to be and never give up on their dreams. In the story, Kate wrote to different gardeners from all over the world to find seeds that would be able to tolerate a desert climate, which reminds me a famous quote from The Alchemist, "When you truly want something, all the universe conspires in helping you to achieve it." I believe Kate's story is sure to resonate with every reader.

Kate Sessions 是一個不被規範所束縛的女孩。她是一個有著大夢想，卻從小地方開始做起的夢想家，她的故事鼓勵了每個想要研究科學的女孩，她的故事啟發了每一個讀者傾聽自己的心聲，她的故事教會了每個孩子成為一個自己想變成的人，不要放棄自己的夢想。在故事中，Kate 寫信給世界上不同的園丁，尋找能夠在沙漠氣候中生存的種子。這也讓逸群老師想到《牧羊少年奇幻之旅》故事中的一段話，當你真心渴望某樣東西時，整個宇宙都會聯合起來幫助你，我相信 Kate 的故事一定能夠引起每一位讀者的共鳴與回響。

3

Do you know any biologist who has made a huge contribution to Taiwan?

你認識哪一位曾經為台灣做出重大貢獻的生物學家嗎？

Dr. Chia-Wei Li, a renowned paleo-biologist and former director of the National Museum of Natural Science, has devoted himself to the construction of Botanic Conservation Center. He dreams to establish a Noah's ark of tropic plants. Dr. Cecilia Koo Botanic Conservation Center was launched in 2008. The mission of the institution is "To conserve tropical and sub-tropical plants in order to sustain the richest biodiversity on Earth." Ultimately, the Conservation Center aims to supply plants for reintroduction into the wild. The preservation of species is a race against time. The survival of these plants and the future of ecologies in Taiwan and around the world are at stake. Dr. Li dedicates his life to the preservation of species. If you have the opportunity to go to Pingtung, don't forget to visit the world's biggest tropic plants conservation center. If Kate Session is the Tree Lady, Dr. Li should be called the Tropical Plants Guy.

李家維博士，知名的古生物學家，前科博館館長，致力於植物保種中心的創建，他夢想建造一艘熱帶植物的諾亞方舟，辜嚴倬雲植物保種中心在 2008 年開始營運，該機構最大的任務是要保存熱帶和亞熱帶的植物，以維持地球上的生物多樣性。最終目標是希望提供原生植物做為復育。保種，是一場與時間賽跑的競賽，其成敗攸關植物的存續、台灣與全球環境生態的未來。李博士奉獻致生所學，投入植物的保育。

如果你有機會造訪屏東，別忘記來世界最大的熱帶植物保種中心走走。如果 Kate Sessions 是樹媽媽的話，李家維博士絕對能夠擁有「熱帶植物爸爸」的美譽。

Photo credit: 聯合報

教學活動

　　《樹媽媽》Katherine Sessions 用一生的堅持將聖地牙哥打造成沙漠中的綠洲，她用以身作則的態度感動了大家和她一起動手植樹。逸群老師這邊提供一個可以和《樹媽媽》繪本結合的教學活動和讀者分享，相信很多學校的導師和逸群老師在開學時，都會對教室綠美化的競賽而煩惱著不知該如何是好，多數老師選擇回家將家中盆栽搬到班上，逸群老師則選擇和學生一起種花植樹豐富自己的生活，帶著孩子跑到花市挑選種子、聽取播種期、扛回培養土、上網搜尋栽種的方式，看著孩子細心的澆水照料自己的盆栽，許多大男孩也有少見內心纖細的一面，班上孩子用自己的雙手打造自己的教室花園，也體會樹媽媽一花一草改變世界的恆心與毅力。

翻攝自：The Tree Lady

The Tree Lady《樹媽媽》
文／ H. Joseph Hopkins
圖／ Jill McElmurry
出版社／ Simon & Schuster (2013)
相關影片賞析／
https://youtu.be/9JmBhL_R-e0
https://youtu.be/ucUSOTyVLZo

With Books and Bricks: How Booker T. Washington Built a School

一磚一瓦建學校

故 事 摘 要

　　從日出到日落，年少的 Booker 都需要辛勤地工作，他必須提水到田野，扛著玉米到磨坊，背著沉重的巨石。Booker 用了吃奶的力氣搬著萬斤的重物，只因為他是個黑奴。Booker 的母親 Jane 是一個黑奴廚師，父親是一個不知名的種植園主。

　　有天，Booker 被他的主人要求扛一些新東西給他的女兒─書本，當他到教室時，他看見黑板上那些奇怪線條所組成的字母，那些字母又組成了文字，他沉重的心情頓時輕鬆不少，他也在文字中發現了神奇的魔力，Booker 想要讀懂這些文字，但這似乎是件不可能的事。

　　在 1865 年夏天，在 Booker 九歲時，南北戰爭終於結束，他的奴隸身分也獲得解放，但他仍需長時間在鹽礦工作以維持全家的生計，Booker 的媽媽也在此時給了他一本 Webster 的拼音書。在生活的壓力下，Booker 一方面勤奮工作，一方面努力學習。16 歲時，他聽說維吉尼亞州有所學校專門培養黑人的學校，但維吉尼亞離

Malden 有 500 哩遠，他只能一路打工賺取車費，前往這所夢幻的學校— Hampton 師範農業學校。

Booker 畢業後留在學校教書，1881 年他在校長 Samuel Armstrong 的推薦下，前往阿拉巴馬州籌建一所師資培育為主的新學校— Tuskegee 學院，當他來到這邊時，他發現了許多對學習熱切的學生，但學校沒有一寸屬於自己的校園，他只能在一個沒有窗戶，屋頂破洞的老舊小屋中開辦教育。

Tuskegee 學院在 Booker 長滿水泡雙手的努力下，一磚一瓦的逐漸成形，他和他的學生自己挖泥、造磚、建窯，在三座磚窯都被燒壞的情況下，Booker 賣掉他的懷錶，做最後一搏，皇天不負苦心人，如今的 Tuskegee 大學已經是所占地 5000 英畝的私立傳統大學。

Tuskegee College
Photo credit: 達志影像

大師觀點／不同視角看繪本

Booker T. Washington 是美國歷史上重要的教育家、作家和政治家，在 19 世紀末 20 世紀初期的美國黑人歷史上扮演著舉足輕重的角色，他主張黑人想要獲得平等的權利，最有效的辦法就是要發展耐心、勤勉、節儉等美德。1895 年，Booker 在喬治亞州首府亞特蘭大發表了《亞特蘭大種族和解聲明》的演說，主張黑人應當接受種族隔離制度，且應當通過自身的努力尋求就業機會。不過此主張也受到另一位非裔領袖 W.E.B. De Bois 的反對，W.E.B. De Bois 主張黑人應該堅持爭取完整的公民權利和逐步增加政治參與，但這並不影響 Booker T. Washington 在美國歷史上的地位，Booker 與白人合作，創建了數百個社區學校和高等教育機構，對美國南方黑人教育水平的提升貢獻良多。除了在教育領域貢獻卓越外，Booker 也在種族和諧及工作關係上也有相當的成就，Booker 更是第一位被美國總統羅斯福邀請進入白宮討論種族問題的黑人。

Booker 是一個出生奴隸的教育家，當他到 Hampton 師範農業學校就讀時，身上只有 50 美分，相當於台幣 15 元，憑藉著決

心與毅力，Booker 半工半讀地完成學業，他也在這所學校奠定了一生事業基礎的學問及為人處世之道。當時 Hampton 師範的教育要求學生注重儀表，皮鞋上油、衣物整燙等對他影響很大，他也意識到黑人要擺脫貧困及低下的社會地位，唯有努力學習，不但要有一技之長，也要有自己的尊嚴。

在看完 Booker T. Washington 的故事後，你是否對學習及教育有了另一番見解呢？逸群老師回憶起自己在大學時，可也是個對學習充滿熱忱的學生，在順利完成企管及英美語文學兩個學位及教育學程後，立志成為一個老師，再成為老師後也透過不斷的進修及研習，精進自己的教學，期許自己成為一個作育英才的教育工作者。我特別喜歡 Booker T. Washington 的一段話：「成功的衡量並不是依一個人在生命中所到達的地位，而是他在追求成功的過程中所需要克服的阻礙。」在這邊和各位讀者共勉。

"Success is to be measured not so much by the position that one has reached in life, as by the obstacles which he has overcome while trying to succeed." — Booker T. Washington.

視像思考／
理解故事脈絡

Who
Booker T. Washington
Where
Tuskegee, Alabama
When
1881

What
When Booker T. Washington arrived in Tuskegee, Alabama, to teach, he found many eager students, but no school. So Booker and his students decided to build their own school-brick by brick.

Conflict
What kind of problem did Booker meet?

Starting life as a slave, Booker experienced the inequities between white children who could attend school and learn to read versus slaves like him who could not.

Character Profile
With Books And Bricks

Reaction

How did Booker react?

When the Civil War ended and slaves were freed, he finally got the chance to go to school and become a teacher. He went to Tuskegee, Alabama, to share his passion for learning. But when he got to Tuskegee, he discovered that the only building available was a tiny shed. So he decided to build a school brick by brick.

Feeling

How did Booker feel at this point?

Booker faced many challenges when building the school. His students were exhausted and wanted to quit, but Booker's passion for learning and teaching inspired them to to continue the exhausting work.

批判思考 / 讀出弦外之音

1 **What obstacles did Book T. Washington overcome to get his education? Which one do you think was the hardest to overcome? Why?**

Booker T. Washington 克服了哪些障礙在他的求學路上呢？哪一個障礙又是你認為最困難的呢？為什麼？

Booker T. Washington had an incredible passion for learning. Born a slave, he didn't have any opportunity to go to school. But his life of slavery changed, the moment his mother got Booker an old Webster's spelling book. He started to teach himself to read. During his study, the hardest obstacle he overcame was the life of a coal miner. While shoveling heavy piles of coal all day, he thought of only one thing — school. After learning that Hampton Normal and Agricultural Institute enrolled black students, he walked and begged rides on the long trip to Virginia. Nowadays, Booker's perseverance and eagerness for learning has become a model for our students.

Booker T. Washington 有著對於學習的狂熱。出生即為奴隸的他沒有任何求學的機會，但他的奴隸生活在他媽媽給了 Booker 一本 Webster 的拼字書那一刻有了改變。他開始自學閱讀。在他一生的求學過程中，他必須克服最大的障礙就是在擔任煤礦工人的那段日子，每天鏟起一堆又一堆的煤礦，他心中只有一個想法：求學。在得知 Hampton 師範農業學校招收黑人學生後，他一路走並搭便車到遙遠的維吉尼亞州。今日，Booker 的堅毅和對做學問的熱忱成為當今學子最好的模範。

2 **The author gives a hint on page 19 about how Mr. Washington can solve his problem with having no money. This is called foreshadowing. What's the hint she gives? (p19)**

作者在 19 頁給了讀者一個提示，關於 Washington 先生如何解決他沒有經費的問題。這在文學中稱為預示，請問她給了什麼提示呢？

The last paragraph in page 19 is "With no money to build another kiln, the teachers told Booker to forget about making bricks. To stop wasting his time. Time." The word "time" here is emphasized twice and is a homonym which means both real time and Booker's pocket watch. It occurs to Booker that he still has a precious watch. Therefore, he decided to sell his pocket watch in order to build the fourth kiln. Fortunately, the kiln baked beautiful bricks. And Booker finally had enough bricks to build a school.

在 19 頁的最後一段寫到，「在沒有錢建另一做磚窯時，有些老師曾勸 Booker 放棄繼續造磚了，停止浪費你的時間吧。」而 Time 這個字在這邊被作者強調了兩次，Time 在這邊也是一個同音異義字，除了有時間的意思外，它還代表著 Booker 的懷錶。這也讓 Booker 想到他有一隻價值不菲的懷錶。因此，他決定賣掉這隻懷錶來建第四座磚窯。很幸運地，這磚窯造出了漂亮的磚塊。Booker 終於有足夠的磚來建造他的學校了。

3 Why do you think Mr. Washington wanted to build a school?

你認為 Washington 先生為什麼要建一所學校？

Born a slave, Booker's studying process was quite tough. He needed to spend every penny he earned on his studies. When he worked as a coal miner, he learned the skill of bricklaying. He used this skill to build a school for everyone to attend. He hoped that students like him could still have an opportunity go to school. At first, all the students needed to squish and squeeze into the tiny shed. When it rained, Booker taught with a student holding an umbrella over his head. He knew his students needed a real building. Therefore, he was determined to build his own school brick by brick.

出生即為奴隸的 Booker 求學之路非常坎坷。他必須把每分他賺來的錢用在求學上，當他在當煤礦工時，他學到了砌磚的手藝，他也用砌磚的技巧建了一所每個人都可以上的學校。他希望像他一樣背景的學生能夠有求學的機會。起初，所有的學生都必須擠在一間狹窄的棚子內上課。下雨時，Booker 一邊教書，學生一面在他的頭頂上替他撐傘。他知道他的學生需要一間真正的教室，他也因此下定決心一磚一瓦地建一所屬於他的學校。

教學活動

　　Booker T. Washington 用長滿水泡的雙手一磚一瓦的把學校蓋了起來，替黑人教育做出重大的貢獻。在逸群老師的繪本課堂中，我也希望孩子們能像 Booker 一樣替台灣的下一代也做出些許的貢獻。因此，我會帶著高中的孩子到鄰近的國小，和這群台灣未來的主人翁說說繪本中的故事，繪本蘊藏著豐富的人文、性別、親情、夢想、歷史與和平議題，希望我的高中孩子能夠將繪本中傳遞的真、善、美傳遞給我們的下一代，一起為台灣的教育盡一份心力。

翻攝自：With Books and Bricks: How Brooker
T. Washington Built a School

With Books and Bricks：How Booker T.
Washington Built a School《一磚一瓦建學校》
文／ Suzanne Slade
圖／ Nicole Tadgell
出版社／ Albert Whitman & Co (2014)
相關影片賞析／
https://youtu.be/07cispyOhWQ
https://youtu.be/hpPkQ9rTBo4

英文繪本讀書會02

繪本英閱會：讓英文繪本翻轉孩子的閱讀思維

2017年6月初版　　　　　　　　　　　　　　　定價：新臺幣420元
2021年9月初版第三刷
有著作權・翻印必究
Printed in Taiwan.

著　　者	戴　逸　群	
叢書主編	李　　芃	
校　　對	JCAB	
插　　畫	Carlos Kao	
攝　　影	Sammy Studio	
排　　版	Lilly Lai	
封面設計	小　草　設　計	

出　版　者	聯經出版事業股份有限公司	副總編輯	陳　逸　華	
地　　址	新北市汐止區大同路一段369號1樓	總編輯	涂　豐　恩	
叢書主編電話	(02)86925588轉5305	總經理	陳　芝　宇	
台北聯經書房	台北市新生南路三段94號	社　長	羅　國　俊	
電　　話	(02)23620308	發行人	林　載　爵	
台中分公司	台中市北區崇德路一段198號			
暨門市電話	(04)22312023			
郵政劃撥帳戶第0100559-3號				
郵撥電話	(02)23620308			
印　刷　者	文聯彩色製版印刷有限公司			
總　經　銷	聯合發行股份有限公司			
發　行　所	新北市新店區寶橋路235巷6弄6號2F			
電　　話	(02)29178022			

行政院新聞局出版事業登記證局版臺業字第0130號

國家圖書館出版品預行編目資料

繪本英閱會：讓英文繪本翻轉孩子的閱讀思維 /
戴逸群著 . 初版 . 新北市 . 聯經 . 2017.06
224面；17×23公分 .（英文繪本讀書會：02）
ISBN　978-957-08-4951-6（平裝）
[2021年9月初版第三刷]

1.英語教學　2.繪本　3.學習方法

805.1 106007268